Sunsets and Shades

Dedication

Dedicated to my perfect little family. Phil (the chinchilla) - Thanks for being the inspiration for Lenny. Parker (the dog) - Thanks for always providing me with snuggles as I wrote. Jett (the bunny) - Thanks for being a constant source of laughter when I started to get stressed. And to my beautiful wife - Thank you so much for being supportive of me disappearing on you most nights so I could write this book. Our life is a crazy one, filled with tons of ups and downs, but there is no one else I would rather be on this adventure with.

Chapter 1: Kinsley

I slowly lifted her shirt over her head and gasped at the first sight of her bare chest. I found myself inadvertently licking my lips as I thanked the Gods above that she wasn't wearing a bra. My eyes lifted to look into those of the woman standing in front of me. She looked nervous, so I took both of her hands in mine and squeezed gently.

"Are you sure you want to do this?" I asked softly.

The look in her eyes suddenly went from one of apprehension to complete and utter desire. "I've never wanted something more in my entire life," she breathed, before crashing her lips against mine.

The kiss was short lived since her lips quickly moved across my jawline and down my neck. A moan left my mouth as she took control, swiftly removing my shirt and tossing it across the room. She discarded the rest of my clothes in this same desperate manner. Soon her lips were back on my body, as if they had never left. My disappointment over her apparent lack of interest in my boobs subsided when I noticed that she had a different destination in mind. She kneeled in front of me as her tongue formed a blazing trail down my stomach. My hands grabbed onto her hair as I directed her the rest of the way.

"Oh God. Yes. That's what I'm talking about." My celebration and focus were both interrupted by a knock on my bedroom door.

"Are you having sex in there, or are you just getting really into your writing?" my roommate, Leah King, questioned from the other side. Before I could answer, I heard the door knob turning, and she was in my room, leaning on my desk.

"I'm just nailing this sex scene. Pun totally intended." I gave her a cocky smile and wink, then made a fist and reached it out toward her. "Celebratory fist bump time. Let's go."

Leah rolled her eyes at me, refusing to give in to my little celebration. "You know it doesn't impress me when you write good sex scenes. It's easy to write about something you know. What impresses me is when you somehow pull off these amazing romances filled with love and mushiness."

I leaned back in my chair and lifted my feet onto the desk. "It's a gift," I bragged, completely aware of how arrogant I looked with the smug grin on my face. I proceeded to lift one eyebrow at Leah. "Speaking of sex. What if that *is* what I had been doing in here, and you had just marched right in?"

Leah waved a hand at me nonchalantly. "You know we don't have any boundaries. I would have survived."

I cackled at my roommate. "You would probably do it on purpose, so you could give your man pointers on how to truly satisfy a woman."

Leah rolled her eyes at me for the second time. "What is it with you lesbians thinking you are like God's gift to sex? Trust me, Liam doesn't need any help in that department. Why do you think I keep him around?"

Honestly, I couldn't figure that out. Leah was gorgeous with her flowing blonde hair, long legs, and piercing blue eyes. Liam always looked like he had just rolled out of bed, and the stubble on his chin just made him look dirty. I wasn't sure what she saw in him, but then again, I didn't understand what any girls saw in guys. I snapped back to the present moment and smirked at Leah. "First off, it's not a thought. Years of research have found that lesbians have better sex lives and a ton more orgasms. I personally take some credit for boosting that statistic. Also, I'm still mad at you for keeping Liam around. You broke our pact."

"We didn't have a pact," Leah pointed out.

I shrugged my shoulders. "I mean it was never explicitly stated, but I thought we were on the same page. Relationships suck. Hookups rock."

Leah took a hair tie off of her wrist and somehow easily pulled her hair back into the perfect ponytail. "Hookups are great, but eventually you meet someone who is worth more than a hookup. I mean, come on, isn't that what all of your lovey-dovey romance novels are about? Girls getting swept off their feet by their princess charming."

Her words made me laugh, even if she was technically right. "My books are crap. I don't actually believe the words I write. I'm just good at stringing them together in a way that makes women swoon."

"Speaking of which - that actually has something to do with the reason I came in here." Her tone made me believe she was about to drop a bomb on me that I wasn't going to particularly like. "I told my childhood best friend that she could come stay with us next weekend and I need you to be on your best behavior."

I cleared my throat and crossed my arms in front of my chest, giving her an indignant look. "Excuse me? Your best friend stays with you every weekend and every other day of the week because we live together."

"I said *childhood* best friend," Leah repeated, adding another eye roll for good measure. "Her name is Grace Harper."

I kept my arms crossed in front of me. "How come I've never heard about this friend?"

"She still lives in our hometown back in Maryland, and we kind of just drifted apart after I moved to Philly. I honestly can't remember the last time I talked to her before a few weeks ago when she reached out to me. She's just one of those people that I'll always be close to no matter how much time passes."

I lifted an eyebrow at her. "And why do I have to be on my best behavior?"

Leah gave me a guilty smile and tilted her head to the side. It was probably her (successful) attempt to look cute in order to soften whatever blow was coming. "So, at some point, I may have mentioned to her that I live with Laurel Lake."

Now it was my turn to roll my eyes. "You don't live with Laurel Lake. You live with Kinsley Scott."

"I know I do, and that's the thing. I love Kinsley Scott. Kinsley Scott is cool and fun and obviously my best friend in the whole world. Also, if the sounds I hear coming through these thin walls are any indication, she's excellent in bed. But Kinsley Scott is also the complete opposite of Laurel Lake. Laurel Lake is every hopeless romantic lesbian's dream girl. Grace just so happens to be the biggest hopeless romantic of them all and also a huge fan of all of Laurel Lake's books."

I huffed my disapproval. "This is exactly why I have a pen name. My own family doesn't even know the name I write under. Sure, that's mostly so my mother doesn't have a heart attack reading my sex scenes, but there is a reason I don't tell anyone, especially girls."

I had done a very good job keeping my identity a secret throughout my career. I was like the literary version of Supergirl. With my glasses, I was the beloved lesbian romance author named Laurel Lake who believed in everything good in the world. Without my glasses, I was the cynical, but realistic, Kinsley Scott. I was the girl who could knock a girl's socks off with one touch, but let's be honest, they were losing much more than their socks. It worked out well this way. The last thing I wanted was for one of my hookups to get the wrong idea and think I was looking for something more.

"So, what you're saying is that you want me to be *Laurel Lake, the writer,* when she's here, so I don't break her fragile lesbian heart?"

Leah's smile grew. "Exactly. She's going through a lot right now. She just got dumped by her long term girlfriend a few months ago, and she's having a really hard time moving on. That's why I suggested she come to visit. She needs to get away from that town for a bit. We're from a small town, and she still runs into her ex, along with her ex's new girlfriend, everywhere."

"Ouch. That must be rough," I replied sincerely. "For you, I'm willing to not be myself for a weekend. You owe me though."

"Of course," Leah answered with a wink, before skipping back toward my door. Before leaving, she turned back around to face me. "Oh yeah. Just one more thing. Under no circumstance are you to sleep with her. I mean it."

I laughed as she made her way out of my room. Why would I ever want to sleep with a girl who thought my stories were anything more than complete fantasy?

Chapter 2: Grace

I groaned as I crammed my car full of more of my belongings. I had much more than I would need for a weekend trip, but I honestly wasn't planning on staying for just the weekend. The thought hadn't even crossed my mind until Leah suggested that I come visit in order to get away for a bit. It had been at least a year since Leah and I had seen each other and that was just in passing. The thought of getting away to the city to spend time with her seemed so appealing, that the more I thought about it, the less it made sense to come back home. Since I was an elementary school teacher, and the school year had just ended, I had a few months to figure out what I was going to do next.

This was very unlike me. I wasn't the type of girl to fly by the seat of my pants. I liked plans and a clear cut path into the future, but it was hard to stay on any sort of path when you find your girlfriend of four years in bed with another woman. It wasn't just any other woman. It was a teacher at the school we both worked at; someone who I happened to believe was a good friend. As if seeing them together for the past six months since catching them wasn't bad enough, I had been forced to move back in with my parents. *You don't really want to stay in a place with such bad memories, do you?* my ex, Becky, had asked. While she was right, it was still heartbreaking that she and her new flame (if I could really call her that since they had been hooking up behind my back for months before I found out) had immediately made *our* place into their own.

I didn't want to see this as running away though. I wanted to believe I was running toward something better. I mean, isn't this how all the best love stories go? Life falls apart to set up the fairytale. I wanted to believe I was being led to Philadelphia to meet the girl of my dreams; however, there was an even bigger part of me still holding onto the hope that once I was gone, Becky would realize what she was missing and beg me to come back to her. In this fantasy, I obviously didn't make it easy on her, but I knew I would take her back in the end. She was my one true love, and part of me still wanted to believe that.

As I began my drive to Philadelphia, my thoughts drifted back to Leah. I hadn't told her my tentative plan of staying in Philly because I didn't want to freak her out. It's not like I was planning on mooching off of her. I was going to spend the few days we planned on and then stay in a hotel until I actually figured out what I was doing. I had a decent amount of savings, and once my mom found out my plans, she wrote me a check for more money than she should have. I tried to refuse it, but she insisted it was a small price to pay for my happiness.

Since my small Maryland hometown was just five minutes from the Delaware state line, my drive into Philadelphia took me just shy of an hour and a half. This didn't seem like nearly enough time to process all of my feelings. By the time I arrived at Leah's apartment complex, I hadn't even considered the fact that I would soon be meeting one of my idols. Laurel Lake was by far my favorite writer. When I discovered her first book 7 years ago (a year after she had published it), I immediately fell in love. I had always been a hopeless romantic, but since her book was the first lesbian love story I read, it felt different. Since I was a complete nerd, I had read books by a bunch of other lesbian authors since then, but her books remained my favorites. She had a way of writing about love that made me never want to give up. Even in my darkest times the last few months, it was her writing that got me through. I had to believe I was on the path to my happily ever after if it started with her. I needed to keep it cool though. The last thing I wanted to do was embarrass myself in front of her.

I found a spot in the complex parking garage, then grabbed my suitcase and used the detailed directions that Leah had given me to find her apartment. I took a deep breath before knocking. A few seconds later, the door was swinging open, and I saw Leah standing on the other side. She immediately pulled me into a tight hug. "Grace-Face! It's so good to see you. How long has it been? A year? Two? Let's not ever go that long again, OK?"

She pulled back from the hug and studied me for a minute, seeming a bit surprised that I was actually standing in front of her. "It really has been too long," I answered. "I can't thank you enough for letting me come visit."

Before anything else could be said, I heard footsteps coming toward us and looked beyond Leah to see Laurel Lake making her way over to me. *Breathe. Breathe. Keep breathing.* Once she joined us by the door, she placed one hand on Leah's shoulder and reached the other out toward me. "Nice to meet you. I'm..." Before she could finish, Leah cut in. "This is Laurel Lake. But I'm sure you already realized that," she announced.

I could have sworn I saw Laurel rolling her eyes at Leah, but the moment passed by so quickly I couldn't be sure. I looked down at our hands and noticed that I was still awkwardly holding onto Laurel's. I quickly pulled it away, wiping my sweaty palm on my shirt. "It's nice to meet you," I stuttered. "I'm Harper...No. I mean I'm Grace. Grace Harper. You can call me Grace-Face. That's what Leah calls me. No. Actually, don't call me that. I don't know why I said that. Just Grace. Call me Grace. Well, I mean, you can call me whatever you want." I cringed as the words left my mouth. *So much for keeping it cool.*

Luckily, Laurel didn't seem thrown off by my rambling. She let out a slight chuckle, that was sweet instead of judgmental. "It's nice to meet you, Just Grace," she said with a wink that made me weak in the knees. I had always known Laurel's words were beautiful, but I never realized just how good looking she was. She had one picture that she used on all of her social media platforms and, if you asked me, it just didn't do her justice. She had straight dark brown hair that fell just below her shoulders and behind her glasses were crystal blue eyes that were easy to get lost in. She stood just a few inches taller than me and had an athletic build. I had to gain control of myself though. It wasn't right for me to be drooling over Leah's roommate.

I was able to collect myself enough to walk fully into the apartment. It was bigger than I expected, with a large living room connecting into a smaller kitchen and a hallway that led the way to two bedrooms and a bathroom. Leah gave me a quick tour in which we stopped in her room to drop off my bag, before heading back to the living room where Laurel had started watching TV. I sat down in the chair the furthest from where she was sitting, hoping the distance would lessen some of my ongoing fangirling.

Chapter 3: Kinsley

We were only two hours into Grace's visit, and I already felt exhausted from this Laurel charade. I was initially pissed Leah wouldn't even let me use my real name around her but then decided it might have been her weird way of trying to protect me. Then again, it made more sense that she was actually trying to protect Grace. Either way, I was stuck playing this part I didn't want to play. I knew it was only going to get worse when the topic of Grace's ex came up.

"So, not to talk about the elephant in the room," Leah spoke more gently than she had ever spoken to me. "But how are you feeling? I know things have been hard since the break-up."

Grace sighed and slid her glasses back up her nose in an adorably geeky way. Even though the girl hadn't done a ton to win me over since arriving, I did have to admit that I found her strangely endearing. She had light skin that was sprinkled with freckles and wavy auburn hair that fell halfway down her back. She had a tendency to avoid eye contact, at least with me, and damn that was cute, even if it did hide those brilliant green eyes away. There was no denying she had the whole sexy nerd thing going for her, but her personality left something to be desired.

"I'm getting by," she said with a small, completely unconvincing smile. "I think I might just need some time."

"Understandable," Leah soothed, while patting her on the knee. "I just can't believe that bitch had the nerve to cheat on you and then make *you* move out."

Grace's head shot up upon hearing Leah's words. "I wouldn't say she's a bitch," Grace said softly. "She's a good person. She just made a mistake. A big one. But still… just a mistake. And we both agreed it made the most sense if I left."

I didn't know whether to laugh or cry at how pathetic she sounded. My tears apparently weren't the ones we had to worry about though. In a matter of seconds, Grace began to whimper and tears streamed down her face.

"Sorry," she apologized. "It's just that… she's not horrible. She was always a really good girlfriend. She's a wonderful teacher. People love her. I love her, but she didn't love me. I'm the one who wasn't good enough. It makes me think there must be something wrong with me."

With this confession, Leah moved closer to Grace and wrapped her in a big hug. The hug only seemed to make things worse, and soon Grace was sobbing on Leah's shoulder. Leah looked past her and over at me as she mouthed *help me.*

I shrugged my shoulders and threw up my hands but was only met with a stone-cold look in response. I slowly stood up and reluctantly patted Grace on the shoulder. "Now, now. There's nothing wrong with you. This is just a minor blip on the way to your happily ever after. You'll see."

Leah tossed me a satisfied grin, and it took everything in me not to start laughing at my own words. Before I had a chance to retreat, Grace turned around and looked up at me with bloodshot eyes. "Do you really mean it?" She quickly stood and wrapped her arms tightly around me. *Damn it, she smelled good. Did she use some sort of lavender body wash?*

Almost as quickly as she had initiated the hug, Grace jumped back. "I'm so sorry," she muttered, clearly embarrassed. "I don't know what's gotten into me. I've just been such a mess lately."

So I've noticed. These were the words that immediately popped into my head. They were the words that I normally would have spoken out loud, but I knew I had to bite my tongue. That was what Kinsley would have said, not Laurel. "It's fine," I lied. "We've all been there."

"Have... have you?" Grace asked shyly. I felt a knot form in the pit of my stomach in response to her question. I didn't have to worry about coming up with an answer though, because Grace spoke again instead. "Actually, forget I asked that. It's not any of my business. Again... I'm... I'm sorry. I'm not normally like this, I promise."

"Don't even worry about it. Some things are better left a mystery though." I threw in a wink for good measure and noticed Leah giving me a subtle thumbs up, clearly impressed with my answer.

"Anyway," Leah cut in, trying to change the subject. "Anything specific you want to do while you're in the city?"

"I thought it would be really neat to see the Liberty Bell." Grace's voice gained some cheerfulness back with these words.

I, in turn, groaned internally. Of course she wanted to see the Liberty Bell. The stupid bell... with a stupid crack in it. I get that it had history and all, but that didn't make it any more interesting. *Really neat* certainly weren't the words I would use to describe it.

"Sounds like a great idea. We could do all of the historical stuff tomorrow, then maybe hit up some bars. Was there a certain time you wanted to head back on Sunday?" Leah asked, quickly adding, "You're welcome to stay until Monday if you want. I'd say you could stay even longer since it's your summer break, but Liam and I are going on vacation."

"I actually wanted to talk to you about that," Grace answered quietly. "I think I'm going to stick around here for a bit. Not here precisely, but in Philadelphia. I thought I could do a short term lease or an extended stay hotel while I figured out my plan."

"That's awesome!" Leah shouted enthusiastically. "I get to spend the summer with my two best friends."

Seriously? Not awesome. I cleared my throat, causing both Leah and Grace to look in my direction. "Leah, could I talk to you please?" I asked, trying to keep my voice as level as possible.

She nodded, and we both made our way down the hallway and into my bedroom. "What the hell are you thinking?" I whisper-screamed, once I knew we were out of earshot. "There is *nothing* awesome about this situation."

A look of confusion and annoyance settled onto Leah's face. "It *is* awesome actually. Grace and I used to be inseparable. She's struggling right now, but she really is a cool girl. If you'd just give her a chance, I truly think you guys could get along really well."

I waved a hand at her. "I'm not sure I believe that, but that's also not the big issue here. *You* told me I have to be Laurel around her. I've been putting on this charade for a few *hours* and I feel exhausted. There's no way I can do this for weeks on end." I took a deep breath before continuing, feeling my annoyance over the whole situation building. "And you know what? I shouldn't have to pretend at all. Grace clearly isn't pretending to be anything she isn't. You said it yourself. You love Kinsley Scott. So I honestly find it pretty shitty that you're telling me I can't be myself."

Leah sighed and looked toward the ground, kicking around a crumpled up piece of paper I had written notes on for my current book. "You're right. It was wrong of me to ask that of you. I panicked, OK? It's hard to bring people together who have known you at two very different points in your life. I was worried you guys would butt heads. But you're absolutely right. I think you're like the coolest and Grace deserves to see that side of you. *You* deserve to let people see that side of you." She finally looked up and placed an accusatory finger on my chest. "But don't let that go to your head. Your ego can't afford to get any bigger."

I laughed, then pulled Leah in close to me, sticking my tongue out to lick her cheek in the process. She pulled back and quickly wiped it off. "That's gross. Why do you always do that? Save that for your special lady friends."

I raised both eyebrows and grinned widely. "I save my tongue for more important duties when it comes to my lady friends."

Leah pushed away from me and shook her head. "You're disgusting." She then started walking toward the door and turned around just before leaving. "Just take it easy on her, OK?"

"Of course. I promise." I tapped my middle fingers together twice, which had somehow become our sacred sign of a promise at some point during our friendship. Leah gave me a satisfied grin, before completely retreating.

Before leaving the room, I switched out my glasses for contacts, then confidently marched down the hallway. I swaggered toward the couch where Grace was now sitting and stopped right in front of her, offering my hand. "If you're going to be sticking around here, I need to reintroduce myself. I'm Kinsley Scott. Unlike Laurel Lake, I don't believe in happy endings. I honestly think love is a crock of shit and you're much better off alone anyway. Sex on the other hand… sex is where you should put your focus. I'm kind of a lady sex connoisseur myself, so if you need any advice on finding someone to bang, I'm in. But I can't be expected to continue to spew this bullshit about happily ever after with you."

Once I was done with my rant, Grace just stared up at me, eyes wide. "That's… good to know." She slowly nodded her head as she spoke. "I'm going to go to bed now."

I watched her as she retreated back to Leah's room, then turned back to look at Leah, who was now shaking her head at me. "What happened to taking it easy on her?"

I shrugged my shoulders. "That *was* me taking it easy on her."

Chapter 4: Grace

"As you can see, this is a picture of the Liberty Bell. There it is in all of its cracked glory. This is exactly what you're going to see in person, only you'll be surrounded by a thousand other people, in a ridiculously hot room that smells like steaming piss and BO. But hey, if that's what you want to do today, that's cool. I'm just warning you. I wouldn't want you to be disappointed."

I looked over at the girl sitting next to me and almost laughed at the irony of her words. *I wouldn't want you to be disappointed.* When I first came out, it was Laurel Lake's books that helped me believe that I could find love. The past six months, her words were my constant motivation to get out of bed and believe in a brighter tomorrow. As if on cue, my phone chimed at that very moment, and I looked down to see a notification that Laurel Lake had tweeted. This time I did laugh out loud. "Good morning lovelies! Any big plans for today? I'm taking a visitor to see the historical #libertybell. Don't forget: it's a beautiful day to fall in love! Don't give up."

I looked between my phone and Kinsley (who was now laughing at some raunchy comedian on TV) a few more times. I laughed again, this time a snort escaping me, which caught Kinsley's attention.

"Huh, Just Grace, I wouldn't have thought you were the type of girl who found this funny. Maybe I judged you wrong."

"Oh, I wasn't laughing at that," I answered, sounding much more shy than I wanted to.

Kinsley raised an eyebrow at me. "Oh yeah? What's so funny then?"

Without saying a word, I held my phone up, which still had her tweet on the screen. Kinsley tilted her head and squinted at it. "I just posted that like a minute ago. How did you…" A cocky smirk split her face when the realization hit her. "You get notifications when I tweet, don't you?"

I wanted to smack the smug look right off of her face. At least, I would have wanted to if she didn't look so cute. It wasn't fair that a girl with a personality like hers had a face like that. What was even more unfair was that body. A body that looked good even wearing her current boxer shorts and oversized shirt from some restaurant with a picture of a pepper and the words *I'm hot* at the top.

"Don't be embarrassed," Kinsley spoke again, clearly referring to the blush that had taken over my face. "I think it's cute that you have notifications on for me. Who else do you have them on for?"

I shrugged my shoulders. "Just a few people." There was no way I was going to tell her I only had notifications set up for two people - her and Becky. Yes, my ex. Apparently, I was a glutton for punishment.

Before this conversation could go any further, Leah walked into the room. She kicked at Kinsley's feet, which were now stretched onto the coffee table in front of her. "Kins, what are you doing?" she scolded. "I thought you said you were going sightseeing with us today."

"I am," she answered, sounding confused by Leah's questioning.

Leah looked down at her watch and then back at her friend. "Well, I told you we were leaving at 10:30, and it's now 10:25."

Kinsley again looked at her as if she didn't know where the attitude was coming from. "I know. I was just about to get ready. Today is a five minute-er type day."

Kinsley followed up her statement by hopping off of the couch and sprinting down the hallway.

Leah laughed and pointed her thumb in the direction of the bedroom. "Just wait. This is actually really impressive."

As soon as 10:30 hit, Kinsley walked into the living room of the apartment looking like a whole new woman. Her hair was pulled up into the perfect messy bun, she had just a slight hint of makeup on, and she was wearing jean shorts with a cute tank top. The most impressive part of her outfit were the lace up gladiator sandals, which probably would have taken me at least ten minutes to put on.

We left the apartment and immediately headed to Independence National Historical Park. Since I loved history, the experience should have been a lot of fun. Only, it wasn't fun because Kinsley spent the whole time switching between complaining and making fun of it.

I had to admit that she was right about the Liberty Bell, but I still thought it was neat to see in person. I was actually relieved once we left the park and headed to a nearby bar, so I wouldn't have to hear Kinsley complain anymore.

I quickly found out Kinsley became louder, and even more bitter and opinionated, once she started drinking. I decided the best way to deal with her attitude was to go drink for drink with her, and as dinnertime approached, we were both pretty drunk. For this reason, Leah thought it was for the best if we headed back to the apartment to eat.

"So, Grace," Kinsley slurred as we stumbled side by side. "Tell me. How long ago did your bitch of an ex screw that other girl?"

I found myself growing irrationally angry at her words. Sure, she could have found a much nicer way to ask the question, but normally I would have just ignored her lack of empathy. Normally, I also didn't drink the whole city of Philadelphia. "I told you she's *not* a bitch" I snapped back.

"Whoa. OK, killer," Kinsley chuckled. "How long ago did you catch your sweet, perfect girlfriend in your bed with another woman?"

Leah moved in between us and put an arm around Kinsley's shoulder. "Hey Kins, remember how you told me to let you know when you were being douche-y? Well, you're being a pretty big douche right now."

Kinsley slipped out from underneath Leah's arm, then moved over to the other side of me, now placing her arm around my shoulder. "She's right. I am being a douche and I'm sorry. I wasn't trying to upset you. I just don't like to see a pretty girl who doesn't notice her own worth."

Twenty-four hours ago if you had told me that Laurel Lake would call me pretty, I would have been ecstatic. But now, I only felt annoyed. "Please don't hit on me," I said softly, while pulling away from her and following Leah into the apartment.

Kinsley retreated to her bedroom, emerging just a few minutes later in the outfit she had been wearing earlier in the day. As she flopped down onto the couch, she looked over at me. "Just for the record, I wasn't hitting on you. Trust me."

"You say that like it would be so hard to believe that you could ever hit on me." I knew I was rocking the boat, and even as the words left my mouth, I wondered why I was acting this way. It was so unlike me.

"Don't get all butt hurt over it," Kinsley huffed. "I meant what I said. You're pretty, and I think you're worth much more than you realize. Still, don't take this the wrong way, but I wouldn't touch that with a ten foot pole." She waved her hand in my direction as she said the word *that*.

I laughed sarcastically, and a snort escaped at the same time. "How am I not supposed to take that the wrong way?"

Kinsley sighed. "I'm just saying. You're surprisingly sexy and while that snort is adorably geeky, it just doesn't do it for me. You're way too emotional, and you take things too personally."

"Is that so? Well, at least I'm not fake."

"Hey guys, I think we should all just..." Leah tried to cut in, but was quickly cut off by Kinsley.

"Fake?! Seriously? How am I fake?"

I scoffed in response. "Seriously?! You hate love, yet you write these big, elaborate love stories. Then, you go online and continue to put on this persona of someone who isn't you."

"That's because it isn't me," Kinsley replied between gritted teeth. "*That* is Laurel Lake."

"Well, if you ask me, it's not fair." I was on a roll now with my body still buzzing from all the alcohol I had consumed. "You're one person online and a completely different person in real life, but do you know what you really are? You're just a disappointment." As the last words left my lips, I placed my hand over my mouth. I didn't know where that came from. Of course, I was disappointed that my idol wasn't the person I thought she was, but calling someone a disappointment was just wrong.

"Well, I don't have to be beat up on by some creepily obsessive fangirl, so I'm going to bed." With those words, Kinsley stormed out of the room.

"Kins. Wait. It's only dinner time," Leah tried to yell after her.

I took in the frustrated look on Leah's face, and it all became too much for me. Without realizing what was happening, I broke down into tears. "Sorry Leah, I think I'm just going to go to bed too. It's been a long day." I gave her a quick hug and headed down the hallway.

As I walked into the room, I heard Leah groan and whisper under her breath, "That went well."

Chapter 5: Kinsley

I awoke the next day to the sound of knocking on my door. Before I could respond, Leah walked in and laid down next to me on the bed. "So yesterday was fun," she said with a sigh.

I held my head as I replayed the events from the previous day. I could only remember bits and pieces, but I clearly remembered arguing with Grace. I felt bad about the fact that I had started the fight, but in just 24 hours that girl had learned how to completely press my buttons. "Look Leah, I'm…"

Leah put up a hand and shook her head, signaling for me to stop. "I'm not sure what happened yesterday, but that wasn't like you. You're not the type of person to get in a drunken fight, then stomp off to bed. I'm not fully blaming you. You were both drunk, and you both said things you shouldn't have. I'm not mad at either of you, but I just want you to realize that it was very unlike both of you. Grace isn't like that either, and she does feel awful about what she said."

She should, I thought to myself. Sure, I had been more rude than I should have, and I did feel bad, but she called me a *disappointment.* That was a low blow.

"Anyway, we're going to the zoo, and I was wondering if you wanted to come. I know how much you love feeding the giraffes."

A smile spread onto my face from Leah's words. "You do know my weakness, but I better stay home and get some writing done," I lied.

"And avoid Grace?" Leah asked, while raising an inquisitive eyebrow.

I let out a defeated sigh in response. "I promise I'll hang out with you guys when you get back, OK?"

"Thank you," Leah answered sincerely, before standing up to leave my room.

Several hours later, when they arrived back at the apartment, I had yet to get any writing done. I had spent most of the day sleeping and playing with my pet chinchilla. Fortunately, the time had allowed me to move on from everything that had happened the night before, and I was ready to start fresh with Grace.

When I walked out into our living room, I found Grace and Leah sitting next to each other on the couch. Grace had some sort of stuffed animal sitting on her lap and when she stood and held it out toward me, I noticed it was a giraffe. "Please take this as a peace offering," Grace said shyly, a slight blush creeping up her neck and settling on her face as the words left her mouth. "I'm really sorry about what I said last night. It's no excuse, but I was super drunk. I normally don't drink like that." When I looked at the giraffe, now sitting in my hands, Grace added, "Sorry. I know it's dorky. Leah told me that they're your favorite part of the zoo."

I wanted to joke around that it was a super dorky gesture, but I had a feeling Grace wasn't the type of person I could joke with. "Nah, it's cute. And she is right - giraffes are my second favorite animals. So I accept your apology, and I'm sorry as well. We both said things we shouldn't have. I have a tendency to egg people on, especially after I've been drinking, and I'm sorry about that. We'll just agree to start over."

"Great!" Leah shouted enthusiastically. "Now that we're past that, what did you guys want to do tonight?"

"I thought it would be a good idea if we..." at the same time the words "went out" came out of my mouth, Grace said "stay in." *Of course.*

I did my best to flash her a smile and through gritted teeth consented, "Staying in it is! You are the guest, after all."

"Awesome." Leah clapped her hands together. "I'll order us some pizza. What kind do you guys want?"

Speaking at the exact same time again, I asked for the meat lovers supreme, while Grace requested plain. *Not surprising at all.*

Leah forced a smile as she looked between the two of us. "Two pizzas it is. Do I even want to ask what movie you guys want to watch?"

I put my hands up in surrender and directed my attention toward Grace. "It's all you, as long as it isn't a romantic comedy, or romantic drama, or literally anything with romance. I get enough of that with my job."

"Oh um.." Grace's hesitation told me that romance was probably the only genre she actually enjoyed. "Whatever you decide is fine."

"Actually, how about we play a game?" Leah suggested.

We finally found something we could agree on, and an hour later we were eating pizza and playing Scattergories. It didn't take me long to realize Grace was the type of person who took games way too seriously. I was competitive, especially in video games, but I still had fun with it. Each time we would begin a new round, I noticed that she would carefully adjust her glasses and take a deep breath before becoming laser-focused on the task at hand. Meanwhile, Leah and I spent more time trying to distract each other than actually focusing on coming up with our own words.

Grace was also one of those people who had the annoying habit of actually challenging answers. After I proudly announced "Pizza" as an answer to *foods you eat for breakfast*, Grace raised her hand. "I'd like to challenge that. Pizza isn't technically a breakfast food."

We both turned to Leah for the final vote. "Sorry Grace. I have to go with Kins on this one. That girl eats pizza for breakfast like three days a week."

Two could play at this game though. When the category of *authors* came up under the letter K, and Grace chose to use my name, I argued it shouldn't count since I don't write using that name. Leah shot me down this time, pointing out that even if I don't use my real name, I *am* still an author.

The game continued this way, with us each finding at least one word to dispute in every single round, becoming more and more out there with our reasonings as we got further along. I knew my argument that Jamie couldn't be used under the boy's name when it could also be a girl's name was crap, but it wasn't any more ridiculous than Grace claiming I couldn't use a certain TV show since it was no longer on air.

Before we had made it through the whole game, Leah threw her pencil down in frustration. "That's it. I'm done. What is the deal with you guys? Neither of you are argumentative people, so I don't understand why you are insistent on fighting each other."

I shrugged my shoulders in response. "Sorry Leah. I just think some people take life too seriously." I tried to keep my tone light to sound like I was joking, although I meant what I was saying.

Grace clearly didn't take it as a joke because a look of disdain quickly surfaced on her face. "And *some* people feel the need to make a joke out of everything. Certain parts of life are serious, believe it or not."

We both looked toward Leah who buried her face into her hands. She stayed like this for a minute, and when she finally lifted her head, she had a maniacal smile on her face that actually had me quite frightened. "I have a wonderful idea, and I'm not going to let either of you say no," she announced. She looked toward Grace first. "I know the extended stay hotel you were looking at was super pricey, and since I'm going on vacation for the next two weeks, there is a free room available here. You'll be staying in that room. This will give you time to figure out a more permanent, or at least semi-permanent, solution. Don't you dare try to tell me no. We both know this makes much more sense financially." Now, Leah turned toward me and pointed a stern finger at me. "And you - you have no say over this. That is my room and my half of the rent, so *I* decide what to do with it." Both Grace and I responded with a slight nod, and Leah leaned back on the couch, a satisfied grin on her face. "You two need to learn to get along, because whatever has been going on this weekend, needs to stop. You're both my best friends, and, yes, you have some very different personality traits, but you've both been super loving and supportive friends to me and you're much nicer than either of you are portraying right now. So, in the next two weeks, you're going to figure this out together."

"Gee Leah, why don't you just handcuff us together and keep the key until we prove ourselves?" I answered sarcastically.

"I thought about it, but then I figured you'd enjoy that a *little* too much." She stuck her tongue out at me, and I slapped her in the face with a pillow while we both giggled together.

When I turned to look at Grace, her eyes were wide, and she gulped audibly. Apparently, this girl couldn't even joke about sex. This was going to be a long two weeks. Correction. This was going to be a long summer.

Chapter 6: Grace

By the time Tuesday hit, I already felt like a prisoner in this apartment. Monday had seemed to drag by, with Kinsley and I doing our best to avoid each other. She spent most of the day holed up in her room, but when I returned from a walk through the city, I found her in the living room watching television. I said a quick hello and tried to ask her about what she was watching, but the conversation just felt forced and awkward. So, I made myself a sandwich and spent the rest of the night locked in my bedroom, which was where I had spent most of this day as well.

It was very unfortunate since it left me alone with my thoughts, and most of those revolved around Becky. Although, there was one other thought that kept creeping into my mind, and I wasn't sure why. For some reason, I kept going back to the conversation between Kinsley and Leah. They had been joking around about the handcuffs, but the whole thing made me feel hot and bothered, which was strange since I didn't ever remember feeling that way before. Truthfully, the expression had always confused me. *Hot and bothered?* Nothing about that sounded comfortable, but people always said it like it was a good thing. While it was a slightly uncomfortable feeling, it was also a nice change to have this burning desire inside of me. *Wait… burning desire about… Kinsley? Kinsley - the girl who treated life (and other people for that matter) as one big joke.* This heartbreak, combined with my lack of any sort of sex life, must have been having an even bigger effect on me than I realized. *Great.*

My thoughts were interrupted by the sound of a notification on my phone. I figured it was probably Laurel

Lake tweeting about *following dreams and never giving up on love*, but I decided to look anyway. That turned out to be a big mistake. The words seemed to pop off of the screen and slap me right in the face. *@teachinbecks11: Check another item off of the bucket list - Hawaiian vacation with my soulmate.* Along with the words was a picture of Becky and Jamie kissing, the Hawaiian sun setting in the background. Hawaii had always been a bucket list item. It was *our* bucket list item. We had been saving money for years so we could afford to go on our honeymoon someday. *Our honeymoon that never happened and probably never would now.*

Before I could stop them, the tears were rolling down my cheeks again, only this time they were accompanied by sobs. I found the remote and turned on the TV, hoping that would mask the sound of my whimpers. I'm sure if Kinsley heard my crying, she would have a big laugh at my expense. After just a few minutes, I heard a light knock on my door. I reluctantly opened it and found Kinsley standing there with a look on her face that I hadn't seen since meeting her. It was a softer look.

She motioned her head toward her room across the hall. "Come with me. There is someone I want you to meet."

I walked into her room for the first time and saw a cage that stood about five feet tall. The cage was filled with so many sticks, toys, and contraptions that I almost didn't notice the cute creature inside. "And who is this?" I asked, surprised to hear my own voice.

"This is my life, my love, my only," Kinsley said proudly. "And before you say it, *no,* he is not a rat."

"I know that. He's a chinchilla, which is in the Rodentia order, but that *does not* make him a rat. It just means he has a single pair of incisors in each jaw and they are continuously growing throughout his life." I paused for a moment, noticing how nerdy that statement sounded. "Sorry. That sounded super geeky. I was really into animals growing up. I always felt like it was easier to figure them out than to figure myself out. I blame it on the whole *confusion over my sexuality* thing. That's easier than admitting that I am just a huge geek."

"Hey, geeking out over chinchillas is always accepted here," Kinsley informed me with a wide grin.

"So, what's his name?" I asked, while I bent down to get a closer look at the little boy who was currently laying in the bottom part of his two-story cage.

"His name is Lenny Lesden Scott."

When I gave Kinsley an inquisitive look, she sighed and added, "Don't ask. Seriously." She then opened the cage, and after only a slight struggle, encouraged Lenny to jump into her hands.

She sat down on the bed and put him on her lap, patting a spot on the bed next to her to signal for me to sit. "Want to pet him?" she asked. I couldn't help but notice the excited look she had in her eyes. It was almost childlike and was absolutely adorable. I found myself smiling in response, which seemed to be something I almost never did anymore.

I slowly ran a hand through his fur, surprised at just how soft he was. "Wow. Chinchillas really are just as soft as they say. I've always heard that, but I didn't know they were *this* soft."

"Sure are, but don't you dare make any other comments about why you've heard about their soft fur. We don't talk about that here, do we buddy?" she cooed at the animal in her arms. I knew what she was referring to. It was the fact that there were actually people who bred and killed chinchillas for their fur - a thought that made me sick.

"This may be a dumb question, but are you ok?" I was surprised by the soft sound of Kinsley's voice, but even more surprised by the feel of her hand gently resting on my knee. When I looked down at it, she quickly pulled it away.

"I am for now," I answered sincerely. "This has been a good distraction."

Kinsley stood up and walked the chinchilla back to his cage, then turned to look at me again. "Do you want to talk about it?"

The surprises just kept coming. Who was this girl? "I'm confused. I didn't think you cared about this. I honestly thought you found me pathetic," I admitted.

Kinsley sighed, then sat down next to me on the bed again. "Listen, I'm not going to lie. I think it's dumb to get caught up on someone who clearly doesn't deserve it. I also think it's much easier to make a joke out of a situation than to harp on it. But, believe it or not, I'm not heartless. I do care if someone is hurting, and I can tell that you are."

I pushed my glasses up on my nose (a nervous habit that I absolutely hated for how nerdy it made me appear) and looked into Kinsley's eyes. Once again, her eyes were much warmer than I had ever noticed previously. "I appreciate that... and I'm truly sorry if I made it seem like I thought you were heartless."

"So, do you want to talk about it?" Kinsley gently pushed.

"Believe it or not, no."

"Well then, we could stuff our faces with Chinese food. But then again, I love Chinese food, which means you probably hate it," Kinsley joked.

"I actually love Chinese food as well. Looks like we found something we have in common. Leah would be so happy."

***

As I ate my food, I looked over at Kinsley who was pouring sweet and sour sauce, not only all over her chicken, but also on her lo mein. When she caught me staring, a smile spread across her face. "What? Is there a problem with the way I'm preparing my food?"

"I was just wondering if you wanted any chicken and lo mein with your sweet and sour sauce," I attempted to joke.

"Oh hardy har. First grade called by the way. They want their joke back." She then lifted the bowl that had the slightest bit of sweet and sour sauce in it and moved it toward my plate.

I put my hand up to block her path. "Don't even think about it."

"Aw come on," she whined. "I'm just trying to make it better. Chicken with broccoli and white rice is *so* boring!"

I ignored her comments and continued to eat. We sat in a strangely contented silence for a few minutes, before Kinsley spoke again. "So, I know of a few comedians that aren't quite as raunchy as the one I was watching the other day. You cool if I put one on?"

I agreed, but quickly learned Kinsley's definition of *not as raunchy* was still a bit much for me. "I'll never understand why people find sexual humor like this so funny," I finally commented when I couldn't take it anymore.

"Oh, come on. Sex is just sex. It's funny to joke around about. It's not like it's anything serious."

"Doesn't it make you feel like you're not respecting the true purpose of sex by talking about it that way? You act like it means nothing. It makes it seem like you would get it on anytime and anywhere with any random person."

Kinsley placed one hand on her chest in response to my words. "Ouch. That's a pretty unfair judgment. I *do* have feelings, you know."

"Do you?" I asked, mostly joking.

"Nah, not really," Kinsley laughed. "But I do have a lot of sex, so I'd say I have a lot of respect for it. I mean the true purpose of sex, as you so eloquently put it, is pleasure, and trust me when I tell you, there has never been any lack of that when I'm involved." She added a wink that brought back the same feelings as the handcuff comment. That quickly subsided once I let her words sink in.

"I disagree," I said with a shake of my head. "I believe sex should be used as a way of expressing the feelings you have for a person that you truly care about."

A look of disgust formed on Kinsley's face when I said those words. "Well, that's just crazy. If you think of sex that way, you'll only have sex with like one or two people your entire life." Kinsley laughed, as though it was a completely ridiculous thought.

"I thought I was only going to have sex with one person for my entire life," I admitted quietly, feeling the sadness return.

To my surprise and disappointment, Kinsley started to laugh again. "Wait a second... are you trying to tell me that you're one of those girls who's saving herself for marriage or something? I thought only straight people did that."

"Well, seeing as how I had sex with Becky, and we definitely weren't married, I'd say that wasn't the case." My tone was much more snippy than intended, so I tried to calm myself down before continuing. "No, I wasn't saving myself for marriage, but I was saving myself for *the one* and I truly thought that was Becky."

"We need to get you laid," Kinsley stated plainly, as if she had ignored everything I just told her.

"I'm not sure how that response makes any sense, given what I just told you."

"It makes perfect sense," Kinsley argued. "You know what they say about the best way to get over someone? It's especially true for you. She has the sex hold over you."

"The sex hold?" I repeated, becoming increasingly annoyed.

"Yes, the sex hold. You can't get over her because she's the only person you've had sex with. Whether you realize it or not, you see that as a bond holding you to each other. You need to break that bond."

I scoffed. "With a random hookup?"

"Absolutely. Random is good. It will stop you from automatically associating sex with love and relationships, hence breaking the hold."

I couldn't help but laugh at Kinsley's words. Since meeting her, this was the most passionately I had heard her speak about anything. Of course it was sex. "It sounds like you've done your research."

"I have," she answered, seriously. "And this is a real thing. Trust me. I'm a writer. Twenty percent of my time is spent writing, and the other 80% is spent researching crap on the internet to guarantee that my books make sense."

I shook my head at her as I stood up from the couch. "I'm going to bed. I appreciate all you've done tonight, but we'll have to agree to disagree on this one. I think we've established that we are two very different people, so I'd say anything that works for you definitely won't work for me." With those words, I walked down the hall toward Leah's bedroom.

"Just think about it," I heard Kinsley yell after me. Unfortunately, that was the problem. I *was* thinking about it.

Chapter 7: Kinsley

On Wednesday night, Grace and I sat in the living room of my apartment eating dinner together for the second night in a row. It was crazy to think that Leah might be right. I didn't expect us to be besties anytime soon, but spending time with her was definitely better than being alone. It made me wonder why we had an immediate distaste for each other upon meeting.

My thoughts were interrupted by Grace's voice. "None of your comedy tonight please. I can't handle that right now." *Oh yeah, that's why.*

"Well, *excuse me*," I joked. "I'm sorry that some of us just don't have a sense of humor."

Unfortunately, Grace didn't crack a smile at my joke, and for a second, I actually thought she might start to cry. "I wasn't always like this," she finally answered, sounding even more timid than usual.

I was going to ask her to elaborate, but it turned out, I didn't have to. "I was never wild and crazy, but I was definitely more carefree. I was silly and fun. I feel like I lost that somewhere along the way. I lost myself."

I took a deep breath, trying to decide how to respond. "Breakups can do that to you."

Grace shook her head in response. "It wasn't the breakup. I mean that certainly didn't help, but I've been feeling this way for at least a year, maybe longer. Sometimes I wonder if that's why Becky found someone else. Maybe I just wasn't good enough anymore."

"That's bullshit," I blurted out before I could think better of it. "I mean, have you ever thought that maybe you lost yourself *because* of your relationship? I realize I don't know anything about it, but aren't relationships supposed to make you a better version of yourself? If yours didn't do that, maybe there were more issues in your relationship than you realized." I paused for a moment, thinking I should stop there, but I was on a roll at this point. "Be honest... was your relationship with Becky as perfect as you're making it out to be?"

Grace only seemed to contemplate this for a brief moment, not enough time to truly consider the question. "It was. At least up until the cheating."

"And you never felt like Becky was holding you back or keeping you from living your own life?"

Grace looked down at the ground and stared absently at her feet for a few minutes. When she looked back up at me, her glasses had slid down her nose, so she had to push them back up. *Stop that. I'm trying to have a serious conversation for once and now all I can think about is throwing those glasses across the room, along with... what the hell? I really need to get laid.*

My thoughts were interrupted by Grace finally responding. "I mean, relationships aren't about *living your own life*. It's about living the life you create together."

I groaned to show my frustration at her cookie-cutter answer. That sounded like something I would post on my social media sites, and I wanted to slap myself for it at this moment. "But were you living the life you created together, or were you trying to live the life that *Becky* created for you guys?"

Grace refused to make eye contact with me, which seemed to be a pretty good indication that I was onto something. "I mean...Becky always had the more dominant personality. I'm naturally more timid. So, it made sense that she made a lot of the decisions. It's just how our relationship worked. It worked for us."

I gave her a look that I hoped would convey that I wasn't buying it. "Are you sure about that?"

"Of course I'm sure," she answered, starting to sound a little annoyed.

I groaned again. She didn't need to be the only frustrated party in this situation. "Listen...do you want to get over this girl or not?"

"Obviously," she scoffed.

"Then you need to do me a favor. No, scratch that. You need to do yourself a favor. You need to stop acting like this girl was God's gift. She *cheated* on you, Grace. Not just once, but continuously - for six months. It probably would have been even longer if you hadn't caught her. I don't care if you were the worst girlfriend in the world, or if you spent the last year and a half of your relationship in some big funk. There is *no* excuse for her doing that to you. So come on. We both know that she was far from perfect." I thought for a moment then added, "I'm willing to help you get over her. But it's going to be *my* way, not the way Laurel Lake would do it. None of that fluffy happy endings and rainbows junk."

Grace sighed. "I don't know. You're not going to make me have sex with someone, are you?"

I laughed in response. "We'll get there. You'll see. But no, I won't *make* you. I have a feeling that I couldn't actually make you do anything, which leads me to believe that you're much more headstrong than you want to admit. Anyway, your first task is to tell me one thing everyday that you dislike about your ex."

"How long do I have to do that for?"

I shrugged my shoulders at her question. "How the hell am I supposed to know? I'm making this up as I go!"

With this, Grace finally cracked a smile. "That doesn't do much to help my confidence in your methods."

I used one hand to playfully push her shoulder. "Do you really have much of a choice?" When she didn't immediately answer, I took that as my cue to move forward. "Alright let's go. Tell me one bad thing about your ex."

"Oh, we're starting now?" Grace asked hesitantly, then sat completely still for a few minutes like she was truly contemplating the question. It took everything in me not to scream over the fact that this really shouldn't have been that hard. "Oh, I've got something," she finally answered. "She and I always talked about how we were going to go to Hawaii on our honeymoon. We were actually saving up money for it. Well, it turns out that she's in Hawaii now… with Jamie… That's the girl she cheated on me with. And I don't know. I just feel like that's kind of crappy. As if they haven't hurt me enough already, did they really need to choose *that* as their first trip together?"

Wow. This girl sounded like a real winner. This was exactly why I didn't do relationships. People are crazy. They are too fickle and naturally selfish to be trusted with someone's heart. "It's not *kind of crappy*. It's super shitty. Like big ol' pile of flaming poop, shitty."

My words brought another slight smile back to Grace's face, and I was honestly just happy that she didn't get mad at me for it. I let the subject drop, and we spent the rest of the night eating Chinese food and fighting over what to put on TV.

Over the next three days, I learned that Becky always had to choose what restaurant they ate at (but only because she was the pickier eater... *gag*), for some reason she hated the fact that Grace wore glasses instead of contacts, and she never actually apologized after Grace found her in bed with another woman, choosing instead to question why she came home so early. I had found out this information over dinner with Grace, which had sort of become our thing. This was still the only time we spent together, but I had a different plan for Sunday.

"Up for an adventure?" I asked after knocking on the door to Leah's bedroom.

Grace came to the door, still wearing her pajamas and her hair sticking in all sorts of directions. She seemed embarrassed when she noticed me staring, but there was no way that I was going to point out that the reason I was staring was because I found it to be a cute look on her. Instead, I left her alone to get ready, and an hour later we headed to our destination, with her looking much more put together but still just as cute.

"So, what are we doing here?" she asked, as we stood in front of the Philadelphia Museum of Art. "Did you bring me here to tell me that the Rocky statue is *just a statue* and nothing to write home about?"

"Absolutely not," I scoffed. "And don't you dare disrespect the city of Philadelphia like that ever again. Nope. We're here because you're going to run up the Rocky Steps, then get a celebratory picture with the statue."

The way Grace's eyebrows came together showed me just how confused she was by my plan. "What am I celebrating?"

Seriously? Did I even want to know if this girl had seen the movies? "Obviously, you're celebrating that you made it up the stairs. That run represents overcoming obstacles to achieve your goals. It's the first step in going from an underdog to a champion."

Much to my surprise, instead of getting pumped from my speech, Grace started to laugh. She was laughing so hard that she snorted, which I was beginning to realize was one of her *things.* "Sorry," she apologized. "I just find it funny when you suddenly become super passionate about something random."

"This isn't random. This is Rocky. Now let's run." With these words, I took off, leaving Grace behind me.

About halfway up the steps, I was surprised to see her come up beside me. Before long, she was passing me, and no matter how hard I pushed, I couldn't catch up. By the time I made it to the top I was out of breath, but the wide grin that had formed on Grace's face somehow made it all worthwhile.

"Did I mention that I did track in high school and college?"

"Nope... I.. think... you failed... to say... that," I spoke between breaths. Once I finally caught my breath, I looked over to see Grace had started to giggle. "Alright, alright. I get it. I'm out of shape. Anyway, next step: throw both hands in the air like you just won an Olympic gold medal." I threw my arms up to demonstrate, and Grace laughed even harder.

"Why on earth am I doing that?"

"Because you're one step closer to forgetting that rotten ex of yours," I said with a wink. Unfortunately, this backfired, and the smile left Grace's face. "Rocky time!" I announced, trying to change the subject.

When we made it to the front of the line for the Rocky statue, I directed Grace to stand next to it and flex her biceps. Instead, she put both hands on her hips. "If I'm doing this, you're getting in the picture with me. I'm not going to be the only one standing here looking like an idiot."

"You won't look like an idiot. Tourist, maybe. Really freaking cool, definitely. But certainly not an idiot," I protested. Yet, I still handed the person standing behind me in line my phone so I could join her for the picture. When I flexed, Grace finally started to laugh again and joined me.

As we headed back to the apartment, I started to wonder what it was about this girl that got to me so much. She was able to get under my skin just as much as she could fascinate me. From what I could see, we were polar opposites, and I wondered if that's what was drawing me in. Either way, I was equal parts shocked and annoyed that Leah's half ass plan somehow seemed to be working.

***

It continued to work as the next week passed by with us spending progressively more time together. By Thursday night, I convinced Grace to go out with me so we could enact the next part of the plan. "So, you want me to just sit here, checking out girls as they walk by so I can rate them for you?" she asked in disgust, as we sat beside each other in a small bar. "Isn't that a very heterosexual male thing to do?"

I shrugged my shoulders. "You have a point. But this is for a good cause, so it's OK."

She rolled her eyes at me as I looked around the bar. "Why do I feel like we're doing this more for you than we are for me?"

I shushed her and began subtly pointing girls out to see what she thought. By the end of the night, I learned that she was into brunettes with long hair and a build similar to her own. "Pretty much, we've learned that you're into me," I joked as we walked back to the apartment.

"Oh, I mean.. I do find you pretty. I just don't think that we could ever.. you know. Or that I could think of you in that way. Not that I think there's anything wrong with you. I just…" Grace fumbled over her words, clearly thrown off by my joke.

"Calm down. I was just messing with you," I joked. Although, it made me feel strangely hurt to hear her say that she could never be into me. *What the hell? When did I start to take things so personally?*

Later that night, after crawling into bed, I heard a knock at my door. "Come in," I yelled, without bothering to stand.

Grace opened my door, and her jaw tightened a bit when she noticed that I was already in bed. "Oh I'm sorry," she mumbled nervously. "I didn't realize you were going to sleep."

"It's OK. I wasn't actually planning on going to sleep right away. I figured I would probably masturbate for a while." I said the words as a way to fluster Grace even more, but now that I had said them out loud, it didn't seem like such a bad idea.

Grace's eyes darted around my room, desperate to look at anything other than me. "Um. Sorry to interrupt. I just wanted to tell you that I decided that I'm ready."

I racked my brain trying to figure out what she could possibly be talking about. When I couldn't think of anything, I simply raised my eyebrows at her in question.

She cleared her throat a few times, as if she was nervous to say whatever it was that she was apparently ready for. "I'm ready to have sex with someone else." Her words came out in one swift breath, and she exhaled loudly after finishing, staring at me nervously while she waited for my reply.

"Hell yeah!" I hollered, pumping my fist in the air to show my excitement.

Chapter 8: Grace

Kinsley and I had just walked into the club, and I was already re-thinking this whole one night stand thing. For a brief moment, it seemed like a good idea. God knows I could use a little bit of physical attention. I hadn't even kissed anyone since being with Becky, and by the end of our relationship, things had really fizzled out between us. I thought we had just gotten busy or too comfortable, but it turned out that she had been getting taken care of by someone else.

I couldn't think about that right now, though. The whole point of this endeavor was to try to forget about her. It was also cute, albeit strange, that Kinsley was so excited about this. I never thought someone would be so passionate about getting another person laid, but I was learning that Kinsley was full of surprises.

"Alright, so there's a whole process to this. We can't just have you jumping in the sack with the first person who looks in your direction." Kinsley's voice brought me back to reality.

"I'm honestly not even convinced that I'm going to be jumping in the sack with anybody tonight, let alone just any old person," I admitted.

Kinsley's smile told me that she believed otherwise. "We'll see about that," she practically sang. "OK... Step one. We need to have you drink enough to loosen up, but not enough to get drunk. You need to fully remember tonight. That's the only way this is going to work."

She walked up to the bar and ordered two mixed drinks, handing one to me when the bartender brought them over. "I need you to drink this whole thing, but not too quickly. This is a gay bar. They make these things *strong*. Even I start to feel it after only a drink or two."

I took one sip, and my throat immediately started to burn. "You weren't lying," I coughed.

Kinsley took an even bigger sip of her own, without even flinching and followed it up with an aggravating, yet sexy, wink. "Shall we head up to the dance floor?" She turned before I could give her an answer, and I had no choice but to follow her.

When we arrived upstairs, I had to stop for a moment to take it all in. Having never strayed far from my small hometown, I had yet to experience a gay bar. And boy, was it an experience. Music was pumping from multiple speakers, and tons of strobe lights flashed all the colors of the rainbow throughout the room. There were boys dancing with boys, girls dancing with girls, and of course, boys and girls dancing together. It was a room full of people free to be themselves, and if I hadn't been on a mission, I probably would have started to cry.

I felt Kinsley's elbow push into my side. "Pretty cool, huh?" She leaned in to whisper. The feeling of her breath on my ear caused goosebumps to rise on my arms. *Great. If I was having this sort of reaction from someone leaning close to me, how was I ever going to make sex last for more than five minutes?*

I started to walk toward the dance floor, but Kinsley pulled me over to the bar instead. "You can't just jump right in there. We need to scope things out," she instructed. "We're going to play a little game of single, taken, or straight."

The game went on until we found our first *victims*, as Kinsley called them. It was two girls who were dancing together, but Kinsley pointed out that the way their eyes were wandering to other girls on the dance floor proved that they were just friends. "The plan is to go dance close to them and then eventually make our move. Just follow my lead, OK?" I nodded in response to Kinsley's instruction since it didn't seem like I had much of a choice.

Unsure exactly how I was supposed to act, I stood in the middle of the dance floor awkwardly bobbing my head up and down and tapping my foot. Kinsley watched my movements and started to laugh. "As cute as that move is, I think you need to lighten up a bit." She took my hands and placed them on her shoulders, then placed her own hands on my hips. The contact made my skin burn. *These drinks really must be strong.* We stayed like this for a few minutes, and I followed Kinsley's lead as we swayed along with the music. When Kinsley moved in close again, the goosebumps immediately returned. "I think we grabbed their attention. It's time to make our move."

With that, she removed her hands from my hips and moved over toward one of the two girls, whispering something into her ear. The girl threw her head back in laughter and soon the two of them were dancing together, leaving her friend alone.

I slowly and awkwardly made my way over to her. When I was close, I reached my hand out toward her. "Hey there! I'm Grace. It looked like you could use some company since our friends are a bit busy." I began to laugh nervously, which was followed by a nervous snort. Luckily, the music was drowning me out, so the girl in front of me had missed my whole awkward ramble. She took my outreached hand and used it to pull me closer to her, turning me in the process so she could dance against me from behind. Even though it felt good to finally have human contact, my eyes quickly drifted toward Kinsley. She had her hands on the hips of the girl in front of her and was moving her body in perfect rhythm to the music. I found my own body reacting more to watching her than it was to the feeling of dancing with someone. I continued to watch as Kinsley moved in even closer and placed her mouth next to the girl's ear. I couldn't tell exactly what she was doing, but a whole new feeling came over me. It almost felt like jealousy, but that didn't make sense. Why would I be jealous? Kinsley had asked me which girl I found more attractive and had purposely approached the other one. As I contemplated this, Kinsley's eyes caught mine, and a smirk came onto her face, which she followed up with a wink. *Great. She probably thought I was checking her out, which I totally wasn't.*

I forced myself to look away and closed my eyes to try to bring myself back to the current moment. Just a few beats later, I heard a familiar voice next to me. "Can I cut in?"

Before I could respond, Kinsley pulled me away from my dance partner and started dancing with me the same way I had just watched her dance with the other girl. The feeling of her hands wrapped around my hips as she danced against me felt *oh so good*. It felt way too good, and I was about to pull away when her mouth was next to my ear again. "I figured I should save you. It didn't look like you were very into it." She then took my ear between her teeth and gently pulled, causing me to feel more turned on than I could ever remember. *Shit.* "I bet you were into that though, weren't you?"

I quickly pulled away from her and rushed out of the room. I forced my way through the crowd and into the bathroom, assuming that was the safest place for me to regain control of myself. *What the hell had just happened? Why did I want nothing more than for that to happen again...and again?* I took a few deep breaths, then splashed some cold water on my face. Clearly I needed to cool down.

As soon as I was out of the bathroom, I felt a warm hand on my arm and looked over to see Kinsley staring right back at me. "Can we go outside for a minute?" she asked, an apologetic tone to her voice.

I nodded my head and followed her out of the bar. As soon as we were outside, she turned to look at me again. "Listen, I'm really sorry that I made you uncomfortable in there. It was supposed to be a joke. Leah and I do weird stuff like that all the time. I guess, for a moment, I just forgot how different we are." *Of course Kinsley would be the type of person to do that with all of her friends.*

I forced myself to finally make eye contact with her again. "Don't worry about it. I didn't mean to get so freaked. You have to realize that I haven't been affectionate with anyone since Becky, so this is all just weird for me."

"Sexual," Kinsley responded firmly. "That wasn't affectionate. It was sexual. I don't do affectionate."

I rolled my eyes at her. "You know what I mean. It's been forever since I've been physical with someone, so I need to adapt."

A smug grin returned to Kinsley's face. "That's exactly why we're here." She skipped back into the club, and I was forced to follow her.

As soon as we were standing by the downstairs bar, a tall skinny brunette made her way over to us. She was wearing tight, black pants and a low-cut, white v-neck that left nothing to the imagination. "Do you think I could buy you a drink?" To my surprise, she was looking right past Kinsley and actually had her eyes locked on me.

When I didn't immediately respond, Kinsley patted me on the back. "I'm going to go find my, uh, girlfriend. You two have fun."

Once she was gone, I turned back to the girl standing in front of me. "A drink sounds great," I smiled. "I'll have whatever you're having."

The brunette motioned for the bartender then held up two long, slender fingers. "Two vodka sodas please." When she passed me my drink, she artfully brushed her hand over mine. "I'm Elena by the way," she purred.

"I'm… Grace…" I muttered, starting to feel ridiculously overwhelmed. Luckily, Elena was easy to talk to and conversation flowed freely between us. After what felt like forever, I noticed Kinsley standing a few feet behind Elena. She gave me a thumbs up, then made a humping motion. At that moment, one of the lights from the bar caught her skin. It was glistening with sweat from dancing too hard. Then there were her eyes; eyes that looked like a vast ocean with the light hitting them just right. My stomach tied up in knots as I stared, and I suddenly had no interest in the conversation in front of me.

"I think my friends are getting ready to leave," I lied. "I better go, but it was really nice to meet you."

Elena pushed her bottom lip out into a pout. "Are you sure you don't want to stay? I could make sure you got home." When I shook my head in response, she added, "Do you think I could at least get your number?"

I shook my head again. "Listen, I'm really sorry, but I'm still getting over my ex. I thought I was ready for this, but it turns out I'm not."

Elena nodded her head like she understood, but the way she quickly walked away without another word told me otherwise. When Kinsley realized that Elena had walked away, she swiftly made her way back over to me. Once she was beside me, she threw both hands in the air dramatically. "Dude, what happened?!" she gasped.

I shrugged my shoulders. "Turns out she just wasn't into me," I lied.

"How is that even possible?" Kinsley questioned. "That girl was already undressing you with her eyes before I even walked away." She shook her head and waved one hand. "Whatever. Forget about her. She's clearly an idiot. There are plenty of girls in this club who would be into you."

"Actually, do you think we can just call it a night?" I felt pathetic to be giving up already, but I was already drained.

Kinsley checked her watch then gave me an exasperated look. "It's not even 11:00!" When I made a face that said I wasn't backing down, Kinsley let out a low growl. "Fine. But you're doing a shot with me before we leave."

After taking a shot that made me go into a coughing fit, Kinsley put one arm over my shoulder and walked me out of the bar. I wasn't sure if it was the shot or the feeling of Kinsley's arm around me, but I couldn't seem to control my movements as we walked down the few steps onto the sidewalk, causing me to completely miss the last step. I was sure I was about to hit the sidewalk face first, when I felt Kinsley's strong grip pull me back.

"Whoa there," she chuckled, as she pulled me up against her. Instead of letting go, she kept her arms wound tightly around me. When she finally looked me in the eyes, her whole demeanor changed. Her eyes softened, and she removed one hand from my back to use it to push a stray piece of hair behind my ear. "I'm sorry we couldn't make tonight work," she whispered. She then cleared her throat and added, "It's a damn shame, because you look smoking."

I stared at the ground hoping she wouldn't see the blush that started to form on my face as a result of her compliment. "I really did want it to happen, but there just wasn't anyone who seemed like the right choice given my current emotional state," I admitted.

Kinsley looked toward the sky as if she was considering my words. "So I have a really stupid idea," she announced, still not looking down. "I'm buzzed enough to suggest this right now, but sober enough to realize that I shouldn't be." She finally looked back down at me. "Ah screw it. I'm just going to say it. What if...you and I had sex?"

My whole body felt like it was on fire just from hearing those words leave her lips. Everything inside of me was screaming yes, which is exactly why I figured I should say no. As if reading my mind, Kinsley put one finger up to my mouth. "Before you say no, hear me out. I promise this isn't me being a creep. The fact that I haven't had sex in like two weeks is only partially contributing to this suggestion. You want to have sex, but you're scared. I already understand your situation. I'll understand if it gets too hard and you decide we should stop. You've already cried in front of me, so if you end up having a breakdown, it's nothing new. Plus, you obviously think I'm attractive, and I feel the same way about you, so I'm sure the sex will be great. But at the same time, you don't have to worry about me breaking your heart. We both have the exact same expectations - one night of mind blowing sex - so there's no questions at all. It will be great. You'll get rid of that sex hold, I'll get to spend a night with more than just my hand, and tomorrow we can go back to being friends, or whatever it is we are right now."

I couldn't help but roll my eyes at her crazy plan. "You act like nothing could possibly go wrong," I mocked.

"Oh I'm very aware that there is a ton of shit that could go wrong with this plan. I'm just too buzzed and horny to care right now."

I wanted to say no. I knew that I *should* say no. Instead, I grabbed ahold of Kinsley's collar and pulled her closer to me. I had no clue what had come over me, and it felt like I was having an out of body experience as I heard the words that came out of my mouth. "Let's say I was some random girl in the club that you decided to take home with you. How would you pull that off?"

A wide grin spread across Kinsley's face when she realized she had won. "Well, I would have started by telling you that you look stunning tonight, which you do by the way, then I would have bought you a drink. Check. Next, I would have danced close to you to make sure you were really turned on. Check, check. I would find some way to bring up the fact that my apartment wasn't far away." I found myself becoming more and more turned on with each word that left Kinsley's mouth. "I would wait for *you* to suggest that we should get out of here, and I would slip an arm around you as we walked out of the club, giving you just enough to make you yearn for more. Even though we could easily walk, I'd call for a ride." With this newest tidbit, Kinsley pulled out her phone, tapped a few buttons, then turned the screen to show me the notification that said our ride would arrive in five minutes. "I'd let you know that it was going to be a few minutes, but I had an idea of how we could keep ourselves occupied. Then I would move in closer, until I was just inches from your mouth." Kinsley did every action as she was describing it, and I closed my eyes awaiting her kiss. Instead, she spoke again, keeping our lips just inches apart so the breaths accompanying her words easily floated from her mouth to mine. "Then I would push you against the side of the building, and I would finally kiss you." I felt my back hit the hard cement and then felt her lips against mine. She gave me a few chaste kisses before taking my lip between her teeth, just as she had done with my ear. This action caused my mouth to open fully to hers as a moan escaped me, and she used this opportunity to allow her tongue to briefly contact mine. Just as I was about to deepen the kiss, she pulled away. "We don't want to miss our ride," she smirked.

It felt like hours waiting for our ride to pull up as the sexual tension surged between us. As soon as we were in the back of the car, I looked over toward Kinsley. "What would you do next?" I asked breathlessly.

Just as I hoped, she leaned across the seat, placing her body partially on top of mine, and began kissing me again. Normally, I would have felt uncomfortable doing this in the back of a car, while a stranger was just a few feet away, possibly taking in the whole show, but I was too turned on to care. All I could think about was the way Kinsley's tongue felt as it danced around mine and how my skin burned as she ran her hand up and down my side. Much too soon, the car came to a stop in front of Kinsley's apartment, and she pulled away from me, my body immediately feeling the loss. Before I could fully consider what was going on, Kinsley jumped out of her side of the car and ran around to open my door. She took my hand in hers, and even this slightest bit of contact had my body back on high alert. We ran through the apartment complex and didn't slow down until we were in Kinsley's room.

She closed the door by pinning me against it, and soon, her hands and mouth were back on me. I made the mistake of letting my eyes drift across the room and paused when they reached the chinchilla's cage. "Do you ever feel weird about Lenny watching you get it on?" I questioned, as Kinsley frantically kissed my neck, stopping only to suck on my pulse point.

"Nah, he's totally used to it," she reassured me between kisses. I continued to stare at the cage as she pulled at my shirt and lifted it over my head. When Kinsley noticed what I was doing, she groaned in frustration and took my hand, pulling me over toward the cage. "Lenny could you please tell this 30% naked girl that you are fine with us having sex in front of you?"

"Of course mom," Kinsley answered in a voice a few octaves higher than her normal tone. "For the record, I am very much OK with the two of you having sex. In fact, I'm not quite sure why you aren't naked yet. Don't let me stop you. I'll probably have a hump of my own shortly."

Before I could say anything, Kinsley directed me over to the side of her bed and motioned for me to sit down next to her. "He's not lying," she said, pointing toward a stuffed animal laying in his cage. "He'll definitely go to town on that thing later. Then once he's done, he'll pull out his dong, which literally reaches the length of his whole stomach and suck on the end of it. They say it's to clean it, but I think he's just giving himself a blowie."

I started to laugh, wondering how we had gone from a hot and heavy makeout session to a conversation about how well endowed the chinchilla was. "So, do you have this conversation with all of the girls you bring back to your room?"

Kinsley began to laugh along with me. "No, actually. This is a first. What can I say? You're special…" She cleared her throat. "I mean you're a special case. I know this is weird and hard for you, so I'm just trying to make it easier on you in any way I can."

I lifted an eyebrow. "You're trying to make it less weird for me by talking about your chinchilla's big penis?"

Kinsley shrugged her shoulders. "Do you have any other ideas?"

"Yes, actually. You could continue what you started," I quipped, while pointing to myself.

I watched Kinsley's pupils dilate as she ran her eyes along the length of my body, before bringing her eyes back to mine. "You asked for it," she growled. "I'm about to devour you."

She left the spot next to me on the bed and straddled my lap instead, wrapping her arms around me so she could unsnap my bra. I let it fall off of me and revelled in the way her eyes took in the sight in front of her. I leaned back in response to her hands exploring my body and felt my eyes roll back in my head as her mouth followed. Soon her hands made it to the button of my shorts, and she looked toward me for approval before removing my shorts and underwear in one swift motion.

She slipped off of my lap to position herself in front of my legs, which I parted in desperation. She sat still for a moment as if she was studying me, and just the feel of her warm breath on me was sending me closer and closer to the edge. "Kinsley please," I begged.

She looked back into my eyes and winked, before finally bringing her tongue right where I needed it. The licks started out gentle, but soon she was sucking and flicking, changing her position and pace in response to the sounds I was making. Sounds that I couldn't believe were actually coming out of me. I had never been the type of person to make any sort of noise in the bedroom, but now I wondered if the neighbors next door could hear us. I put my hands in Kinsley's hair, forcing her even closer to me and lost control as her tongue dipped inside of me. Kinsley held me close as I rode out my orgasm and let go only after I fell back onto the bed.

She wasted no time standing up and stripping off her own clothes. Before I could fully comprehend what was happening and drink up her body, she was pushing me further back onto the bed and crawling on top of me. Finally, she leaned down and placed one hard kiss on my mouth, before pulling back again. "Buckle up," she teased. "We've got a long night ahead of us."

Chapter 9: Kinsley

I woke up Saturday morning feeling completely refreshed, which was strange given that I had just gone to sleep three hours before. I had to hand it to Grace. She had handled our marathon sex night like a pro. She had quite a large amount of endurance, especially given how long it had been since she last had sex. Also, for someone who was so vulnerable, she didn't let her emotions get the best of her. We had our fun, many times over, and when neither of us had any energy to continue, she slipped out of my bed to go back across the hall to Leah's room. It was surprising, to say the least. I was sure she would try to cuddle me and had decided I would be OK with it, just this once. When it didn't happen, there was a part of me that felt strangely disappointed. It was probably the part that was holding out hope for morning sex. We had made the decision that we would have sex one night only, so waking Grace up to go for another round (or five or six) would have gone against our deal. I had to admit that it was tempting though.

Instead, I decided to go to the kitchen and start making breakfast. I had worked up quite the appetite and had a feeling that Grace probably did as well. Soon, I was preparing a feast of eggs, bacon, sausage, and toast. I was dancing around the kitchen when I heard footsteps coming up behind me. "Making breakfast?" Grace asked, while snagging a piece of bacon. "Be careful, Kinsley. I don't think you're supposed to make breakfast for a one night stand. You could give a girl the wrong impression."

I chuckled as I continued to prepare the eggs. "I don't know what you're talking about. I came home last night and went right to bed. Nothing else happened. There was no screaming or bedrocking; Certainly not multiple, earth-shattering orgasms."

When I finally turned around to look at Grace, I noticed that, although she was currently smiling, her eyes were bloodshot with red rims around them. I felt my stomach drop immediately. "You were crying," I pointed out like an idiot.

Grace took off her glasses and rubbed at her eyes. "It's honestly nothing. I got oddly emotional after everything last night, but it had nothing to do with you. I promise. It's just some stuff I have to work through. All part of the moving on process."

I continued to stare at her, unsure of what to say. I didn't do emotions. This was exactly the type of thing I tried to avoid. But then it hit me: I could avoid this. Grace was giving me an out. She wasn't forcing me to listen to her moan and groan about how heartbroken she was. So, I simply shrugged my shoulders and muttered, "Alright, if you say so," wondering why it hurt to think of Grace crying in bed alone.

The room went silent for a few minutes before Grace finally spoke again. "Thank you by the way… for… last night. You were right. I needed that. And even though these past two weeks have been a complete rollercoaster ride with us, I'm still glad my first time back was with you and not someone random. So… umm… yeah… thanks."

Once Grace was done rambling, I immediately broke into laughter. Soon *I* was the one crying. When I noticed Grace wasn't laughing along with me, I forced myself to stop. "Sorry. It's just that no one has ever *thanked* me for sex. Which, come to think of it, is quite shocking, actually. They should be thanking me after the way I get them to scream out my name."

Instead of laughing, Grace scrunched up her nose in disgust. "Gee Kinsley, you really know how to make a girl feel like she's just another notch in your bedpost. How nice of you."

I watched her face, waiting for her to crack a smile and tell me she was just kidding, but the longer I stood there staring, the more angry she seemed to get. Apparently, unless I said something, we were just going to spend the whole day glaring at each other. "Dude, it was a joke. Chill out."

Clearly these were not the right words because Grace responded by huffing loudly before turning away from me. "Not everything is a joke, Kinsley. Some things should be taken seriously."

"Fine, Grace, whatever you say," I responded sarcastically, before lowering my voice and adding, "So much for being more carefree."

I looked over at Grace just in time to see her face turn five shades more red. I couldn't tell if she was going to attack me or breakdown into tears, and I honestly wasn't sure which would be worse. Just when I was starting to get along with this girl, she had to go and ruin it once again.

"Screw you, Kinsley!" Grace finally shouted, much louder than necessary if you ask me.

"We already tried that last night, and that's what started this stupid fight," I retorted.

This time a couple of tears did come to Grace's eyes. She used her forearm to wipe them away, before staring daggers at me again. "Just forget about the stupid sex, ok? Forget that I ever thanked you for it. We'll just pretend it never happened and never talk about it again."

"GOOD!" I yelled, throwing my hands in the air to emphasize how done I was with this conversation.

"Good," Grace repeated more quietly, before turning on her heels to march back down to Leah's room.

I followed suit and slammed the door as I retreated into my room. For the next few hours, I sat at my desk trying to write but couldn't get any words down. *Great. Not only had I been forced to hide out in my room, but now, I also had massive writer's block.* I slammed my computer shut, then stood from my desk and walked to Lenny's cage. I opened the door and bent down so he could hop onto my shoulder. He scurried across my back, and I sat on the bed, so he could jump off of me and run around. As I watched him on the bed, my mind flashed back to the activities from the night before. My body felt like it was on fire as I thought about my body on top of Grace's, the way my hands felt touching her, her hands touching me... *Great. Now I was getting turned on all over again.*

As Lenny jumped on my lap, I smiled down at him. "Girls are crazy man. Stick to your inanimate object." I paused as if I was giving him a chance to reply, then sighed at his unspoken words. "I know. I was *kind of* a jerk. I do feel bad about that. But she still didn't have to get so angry."

We sat like this for a few more minutes before I finally put him back in his cage and dared to venture into the living room. The room was dark and quiet, so I turned on some sports show and half listened as I let my mind drift elsewhere. I'm not sure how much time passed before I heard a door open down the hall. A few moments later, Grace sat down on the couch next to me.

"So, you know that thing we're not talking about? I think we should continue to not talk about it, but I just wanted it to be known that I'm still glad it happened. I don't regret it, and I don't want to forget about it. Also, for whatever reason, I've really missed hanging out with you this afternoon, so could we go back to being cool?"

A smile formed on my face in response to her words - one that felt much goofier than I would have preferred, if I could have controlled it. "Of course we're cool," I reassured, giving her a playful punch in the arm for good measure. "I *am* sorry though. I shouldn't have said what I did. I need to realize that some people just don't have the same sense of humor as me and not to make stupid jokes that are hurtful. You're not just a notch. I promise."

Grace pursed her lips together, but I could tell she was trying not to smile. "It's strange when you're nice. It kind of creeps me out."

I crossed my arms in front of my chest in mock indignation. "Fine. If you don't want me to be nice, I won't." Before she could react, I dug my hands into her sides and began tickling her. I was happy to discover that she was indeed ticklish.

She gasped for air between fits of giggles and did everything in her power to squirm away from me. "Stop... that... now.." she breathed. "No... one... likes... that..."

"Funny. It sounds to me like you're really enjoying it," I joked, but truthfully, *I* was the one who was enjoying it. I would have used any excuse to get my hands back on Grace, and it felt good to have her below me, even if it was in a totally nonsexual way. Also, I was learning that I liked watching Grace lose control. She was normally so straightlaced and put together that watching her let loose was sublime.

"Well, I'm totally not," she pouted, trying to loosen herself from my grip so she could push me away.

"Fine," I conceded, removing my hands from her stomach and placing them on either side of her. "But only because that pouty face is so darn cute." Instead of moving, I stayed in position, hovering above her, our bodies just inches apart in so many places. My eyes scanned her body, then stopped on her lips, and my mind was immediately taken back - back to how good she looked totally exposed in front of me. Back to the way her lips moved against mine. Back to the sounds she made as she fell apart in response to my touch - sounds that I longed to hear right now. I forced myself to look into her eyes, only to be more turned on when I realized her eyes were already on my lips, clearly contemplating her next move. It would have been so easy to take her right here. I wanted nothing more than to have my way with her right here on the couch. I knew I couldn't let that happen though. The night before had been a one time thing. If it became more than that, I might be giving her the wrong idea, and the last thing I wanted to do was to break her heart all over again when I was trying to help her put it back together.

I reluctantly pushed myself up and away from her so I was sitting in an upright position on the couch. That wasn't enough though. I could still feel the heat radiating between us, so I jumped up in order to create even more space and hopefully extinguish the flames of lust.

"How about breakfast for dinner?" I finally blurted out, unsure what else to say. I rushed to the kitchen and began pulling tupperware out of the refrigerator. "I have a lot of leftovers from this morning since you stormed off without eating." Unable to deal with any brief moments of silence, I continued to ramble. "You probably don't do breakfast for dinner, do you? Too out of the ordinary for you, right? I could get us something else."

"Breakfast for dinner sounds great." I followed the sound of Grace's soft voice and found her leaning against the doorway to the kitchen. She wasn't smiling, but she also didn't seem flustered or upset. She simply looked content, and it took everything inside of me not to yell at her for it. She looked downright flawless leaning against the wall, not seeming to have a care in the world. *Why was this happening to me?* Sex never had this sort of effect on me. Granted, it was great sex, but still.

I cleared my throat and forced myself to look away. "By the way, I don't think we should tell Leah what happened."

"Of course," Grace agreed. "It's our little secret."

***

Keeping this secret seemed like it should have been an easy task. That was until Leah barrelled through the door the next day and found Grace and I laughing over a commercial on TV. "Hold up," Leah gushed, as she looked back and forth between the two of us. "Did my plan *actually* work? Well shit." I wanted nothing more than to slap the sly grin off of her face, but she was right. Technically, it did work.

"I still think it would have worked better if you went with my handcuff plan though," I joked.

"Yuck," Grace scoffed playfully. "You wish." She then shoved her shoulder into mine, and when our eyes met, they lingered on each other.

Our moment was interrupted by Leah clearing her throat. "Kinsley, do you think we could have an emergency roommate meeting?"

"Sure thing boss," I chortled.

As soon as we were in my room, she closed the door behind us, then turned to look at me, eyes burning through me in a way that made me start to sweat. She looked like she was ready for an interrogation, and I was never great under pressure. "So, what's up?" I stuttered, trying my best to keep my cool. I had never once flat out lied to Leah, and I wasn't sure how I was supposed to start now.

Leah crossed her arms and began tapping her foot, tilting her head slightly to one side and raising both eyebrows. "I don't know Kinsley. You tell me. What's going on with you and Grace? What the heck happened when I was gone?"

I quickly tapped my middle fingers together, then shook my head. "Nothing. We just became friends. You were right. Once we actually put in effort, we learned to get along. That's all."

Leah stared down at my hands, eyes wide. They stayed wide as they drifted up to look into mine. "You triple tapped. You freaking triple tapped. You know how sacred a double tap is and would never lie on that." Her voice became louder and more rushed as she spoke, then she brought her hand up to her mouth. "Oh my God. You slept with her," she added more quietly.

"I mean I wouldn't exactly call it that."

Leah sucked in her bottom lip and continued to stare right through me. "Oh yeah? What *would* you call it?"

"Helping out a friend?" I shrugged. "You saw her. She was having a hard time. I was trying to help her move on."

Leah shook her head at me again. "Geez, Kins. You help your friend move on by listening to her and giving her a shoulder to cry on, not by giving her an orgasm."

"Multiple"

"What?"

"There were multiple orgasms."

Leah covered her face with her hands, and even though she wanted it to seem like she was mad, I knew her well enough to know that she was laughing. "For God's sake, Kinsley," she chuckled. "What does this mean for the two of you?"

"Absolutely nothing. It was a one and done." I looked into space and chortled as my mind drifted again. "Well, *technically,* it was a couple and done. I'd say at least five. Possibly ten. Maybe even more. To be honest, I lost count."

Leah put a hand up to motion for me to stop talking. "Ok. I don't need to hear about how many orgasms my two best friends gave each other. There are more pressing matters right now. Like the fact that I was going to ask about letting Grace stay with us for awhile until she gets back on her feet, but now I don't know how that will work with this new development."

The idea of Grace staying with us excited me. Even without the sex, I happened to enjoy how she kept me on my toes. There was something kind of sexy about not knowing when a girl was going to flip out on you next. I didn't want Leah to realize how much I liked the idea though because I was worried that might change her mind. "I think we could make that work," I answered nonchalantly. "We've been very well behaved since Saturday morning. I mean, there was the one almost slip up on the couch, but aside from that, we were the perfect roommates."

Leah simply rolled her eyes at me, then turned around. "Fine. Let's go talk this over with Grace. But if this all blows up, it's your ass that's on the line."

"Fine by me," I agreed. "But could you do me a favor and not tell Grace that I told you this? I kind of promised it would stay between us."

"No problem, Kinsley. I won't say anything." She reached out and took ahold of the doorknob, but before turning it she paused. "By the way, what the hell happened on our couch?" she asked, sounding disgusted.

"Nothing at all. I said *almost* slip up."

Leah nodded, then proceeded to walk down the hall. When she was a few feet ahead of me, I added, "But if you have a problem with something like that happening on the couch, you might want to buy a new one. Just saying."

I watched her shudder at my words, and I grinned from ear to ear as I followed behind her. Once we were back with Grace, Leah explained the plan.

"That's really nice, but where would I sleep?" Grace asked.

"Well, I don't mind sharing my bed, so you can just sleep with me. Plus, I spend a lot of nights over at Liam's, so you'll practically have the room to yourself."

Grace looked between the two of us, seemingly searching for any signs of reservations, and when she didn't get any, a sweet smile settled onto her face. "That would be great guys. Thank you. I really appreciate that you would do this for me."

"You know, there is one other option. You could always sleep in Kinsley's bed. Although, I'm not sure how much sleep you guys would get, unless, of course, you somehow learned how to keep it in your pants." My eyes went wide at her words, but Leah simply gave me a cocky half smile. "That's for the couch."

Chapter 10: Grace

I wasn't sure how I was ever expected to fall asleep with Leah shaking from laughter beside me. "I just can't believe that my cute innocent little Grace-Face - the girl that used to cover her eyes when people kissed in movies - had a night of marathon sex with *Kinsley Scott*."

I covered my face with my hands as I felt it getting red. "Seriously, what did she tell you?!"

"Believe it or not, she was very respectful. She didn't tell me much at all."

I actually did believe it. I could tell that Kinsley felt bad about Leah finding out, but from what I could gather Leah kind of backed her into a corner. To be honest, I was kind of relieved Leah heard it from her. I am a terrible liar, who is just as bad at lying by omission, so it was only a matter of time before I broke down and told her myself. Now, I didn't have to worry about that being the cause of another inevitable fight between Kinsley and I.

I was brought back to the present moment by Leah elbowing me in the side. "I'm not sure if I actually want to know this, but how was it?"

"It was… good," I answered hesitantly. How was I supposed to be honest with her? I couldn't tell her that I've never experienced sex like that in my entire life. That I didn't know it was possible for sex to feel that way. There was no way that I was going to admit that just thinking about it now had my heart beating faster. "It was *really* good," I sighed, surprising even myself when the words were said out loud.

"Whoa. You need to do me a favor and never tell her that. Her head is big enough already."

I could feel my face turning red in response. "I don't think I did a very good job of hiding it," I admitted.

"Girl, given the noises I've heard coming from that room, I don't think most people do." Leah's words caused a heavy feeling to settle in my stomach. Of course I knew that Kinsley had a very active sex life. She didn't do anything to hide that fact. That still didn't mean that I enjoyed thinking about it though. Leah must have read something in the look on my face because she reached out and grabbed my hand. "Listen. Are you OK with all of this? I know Kinsley can be very persuasive, but once she gets what she wants, she normally moves on. I'm not faulting her for it. It's her life, and she is free to live it the way she wants. I just want to make sure that you won't get hurt through all of this."

"I'm good, Leah," I smiled. "I wanted it just as much as Kinsley did, maybe even more. I know exactly where we stand. It was a good time. She was a good time. That's all that matters."

"Good, good," Leah sighed contentedly, finally drifting off to sleep.

The next morning when I awoke, my "good time" was in the kitchen making breakfast. Leah was right behind me as we left the bedroom and lifted her nose in response to the smell. "What's the occasion?" she asked as we closed in on Kinsley. Kinsley, who had her back to us - her racerback tank showing the full definition of her muscular back. I thought about the way those muscles looked when she wasn't wearing anything; how perfect it felt with her athletic build overtaking my body; the way my hands seemed to burn as they explored every inch of her. *Great.* The whole point of having sex was to try to get rid of certain feelings, and now, I was feeling more than I had in a really long time. At least this was a different type of feeling. Lust was much better than heartbreak.

The burning desire in my stomach grew as Kinsley turned and smiled at us. "I'm just trying to be nice and take care of my roommates."

"From the sound of it, you already did that," Leah jeered, earning her a glare from both Kinsley and I.

Leah ate her breakfast quickly, then rushed off to get ready for work, leaving just Kinsley and I at their small kitchen table. "So, I have to spend the next few hours working on my novel and a few freelance articles, but then I want to enact the next step in 'Operation Love Sucks'" she announced, not taking the time to actually chew the food in her mouth before speaking.

I raised an eyebrow at her. "That's what we're calling it now? Really? Also, why don't you try finishing your food before you talk?"

Kinsley stuck out her tongue that was currently piled with half-chewed food from her latest bite. "You mean this food?" She took a large sip of orange juice, then looked back at me, seriously. "I'm about to ask you a question, and you need to not lie to me."

I gulped audibly. *Please don't ask me anything about the sex. Please.* "Ok..."

"I know you brought a lot of stuff with you from home. Did you bring anything related to Becky?"

Another gulp. "Oh. Umm...No. I mean...not exactly. We were together four years, so of course, there are certain *things* that were ours that are now mine. But nothing..." As Kinsley stared me down, I felt my hands start to sweat. She was seeing right through me at this moment. "Fine. There may be a box," I added.

A half grin surfaced on Kinsley's face. "A box, huh? Filled with mementos of your love?"

I looked down at my plate and began pushing the food around with my fork. "Something like that..."

"Perfect! Bring it in here, and meet me in the living room around 3:00!" Before even letting me answer, Kinsley grabbed both of our plates, put them in the sink, and walked back to her room.

At 3:00, I sat in the living room with a large box sitting in front of me - one that I hadn't dared to look at for the past three months. The first three months of our breakup had been spent with me looking at it almost every day, poring over every word of every single note, wondering where it went wrong.

"Well, shit," Kinsley laughed, as she sat down next to me. "I didn't think you would have *that* much. Did you seriously not get rid of anything?"

I shrugged my shoulders, unwilling to admit that I truly hadn't. I could only imagine how hilarious Kinsley would find that and found myself getting angry over that fact. She couldn't possibly understand. She never would.

"It's OK," she said more softly. "This just makes today's task even better." She opened the box and picked up a tiny stuffed bird. It was a prize that Becky had won me from a claw machine the very first summer we were together. We had made a trip to the beach and… I was brought back to reality by the sound of ripping fabric and saw my bird, in two pieces, sitting in Kinsley's hands.

"What the hell did you do that for?!" I spat. Who did this girl think she was? Did she really think that just because we had amazing sex, now she had the right to do whatever she wanted to my personal property?! Oh no. This wasn't OK.

"I'm destroying everything that reminds you of your ex. Well, I just did this one. You'll take care of the rest. It's therapeutic. Trust me." There was a wide grin on her face as if she had no clue that what she was doing was wrong.

"Oh yeah? And how would you know that it's therapeutic?! I'm not sure how you suddenly labeled yourself the master of moving on."

A look came onto Kinsley's face that I didn't recognize. Hurt? Anger? I wasn't sure. At this moment I honestly didn't care because I was still fuming over the poor decapitated bird lying on the floor. "You know what? I was just trying to help. But if you don't need my help, that's fine. Keep holding on to all of this shit. See where that gets you." Without another word, she stood up and stormed out of the room. Just a few seconds later, I heard her bedroom door slam shut.

I stared down into the box in front of me and tears came into my eyes as I pulled out the first note. It was a small piece of paper that simply said, *"Coffee tonight? - BC."* I remembered this note perfectly. That trip for coffee was what Becky and I always considered our first date. My first year out of college had been spent substitute teaching in a bunch of neighboring school districts. I noticed Becky the very first time I subbed at my old elementary school. She had confidence radiating from every pore, and I found that so attractive. Of course, she didn't notice me. It took countless times subbing at the school and many stupid excuses, on my part, to stop by her room before she even remembered what my name was. By the time I got a full time job at the school the following year, we had become acquaintances. That quickly blossomed into a friendship when we discovered that we were both gay.

I always knew that I was attracted to Becky, but I didn't know how she felt about me. That was until the day this note was slid under my classroom door during my free period. I obviously accepted her invitation, and we spent hours in that coffee shop, talking about our lives and our dreams for the future. She stole my heart that day, and I always thought that would be the story that we told to our children and grandchildren.

I placed that note on the floor and grabbed another one out of the box. I had to wipe my tears away so I could actually focus on it. This note was written on a piece of computer paper and looked like one that she would have left for me on her pillow or on the nightstand if she got up before me. *"Happy December 1st baby!! It's almost time for Christmas. I love spending holidays with you, and I'm so excited that we get to spend every holiday (and every other day) together for the rest of our lives."* I also recognized this note right away. This one wasn't hard to remember since it had just been written this past December. Just 27 days before I caught her in bed with another woman. She had written me this note knowing that she was in the process of falling in love with someone else (or possibly already in love if I went by the timeline she gave me after the breakup). She hopped out of our bed early that morning, with the story that she had some sort of planning meeting. This was really just code for morning sex with her other woman, and she had the nerve to write me a note about spending the rest of our lives together.

In the months following the break up, I had read this note over and over again as proof that she really did care. She *did* love me. She wanted to spend her whole life with me. She had written it plain as day. I figured that this note was the truth and everything else that had happened had just been a mistake. *This* was the real Becky. That girl who cheated on me and then tried to tell me that she hadn't been in love with me for at least a year wasn't her. But, as I read it now, I saw it in a different light. She didn't want to be with me. She had found someone else. Yet, instead of telling me the truth, she had decided to string me along. Why was that? Was it just in case things didn't work out with her new love?

If I hadn't caught them, how long would it have continued? Would I still be living in this messed up world where I believed I was with my soulmate, as she gave herself completely to someone else?

My sadness turned into anger, and I ripped the note apart. Then, I turned to the other note that was already sitting on the floor and tore that apart as well. Man, Kinsley was right. This felt great. Oh. *Kinsley was right.* I gathered the ripped pieces of paper into my hands and marched over to her room, using my elbow to knock so I didn't drop anything. When Kinsley opened the door, I dropped the pieces in front of her. She looked from the ripped paper and then up at me, confusion present in her eyes. Instead of saying anything, I threw my arms around her. I tried to ignore the feeling resonating in the pit of my stomach when she hugged me back, pulling me in close and breathing into my hair.

We stayed lost in this embrace for what felt like forever, until I forced myself to pull back, immediately missing her touch. "You were right, and I'm sorry," I apologized.

Kinsley simply chuckled in response. "I'm sorry too. I probably shouldn't have just killed a stuffed animal without asking you if it was OK."

Her laugh brought a smile to my face, and I hoped that I wasn't also blushing. "Benny the bird totally deserved to die." I hesitated, then added, "I'm ready though. Are you still willing to help me?"

Kinsley's smile grew even bigger. "Hell yeah. I love destroying stuff."

And destroying stuff is exactly what we did. For the next two hours, Kinsley and I made our way through the box, cutting, ripping, stomping, and even setting on fire (her idea, not mine) all of the items. I thought I would be sad to finally let go of all of my memories of Becky, but that wasn't the case at all. I felt invigorated. By destroying those memories, I was also destroying everything that was trying to hold me back. I didn't want to be held back anymore. I was ready to move forward.

As I pushed the mangled contents of the box down the apartment's trash chute, Kinsley put an arm around me. "Doing ok?" she asked sweetly.

"I'm doing better than OK, actually." I took the opportunity to lean in close to her, relishing the feeling of her strong, protective arm around me.

"Good. Because the next thing I have planned is even better than this." *Oh no…*

Chapter 11: Kinsley

"What is this place?" Grace moaned, as I parked in front of a building that looked like an old abandoned factory.

"Just wait," Leah answered before I could.

Grace crossed her arms as she looked between us, and then over to Liam, trying to get an answer, but none of us spoke. The way she pouted was so adorably annoying that it was totally worth keeping it a secret. "I don't understand why you all get to know what we're doing and I don't."

Leah shrugged her shoulders. "I honestly don't get it either. But Kinsley threatened to cut Liam's balls off if we told you."

I rolled my eyes at both of them. "That's because I was afraid she would say no if we told her what we were doing."

Liam hopped out of the back seat of the car like a giddy school boy. "I don't see why anyone would say no to this. It's going to be awesome!"

As we all walked toward the building, I had to admit that this certainly wasn't the type of thing that I would normally be doing on a Saturday night. Normally, I'd be at a gay bar trying to pick up a girl and not… "Ax throwing?!" Grace read after we walked into the building. "I'm not sure why you thought I would say no to this. It sounds awesome!"

Hmmm... apparently I had misjudged her. I tended to do that a lot with Grace. Although she seemed to be an open book, there was much more to her than initially meets the eye, and I found that super sexy. Ever since we had sex a week ago, I was finding more and more about her to be irresistible. That would have been concerning for me if I didn't feel like we were on the same page. But we totally were. We were friends. Friends that enjoyed arguing and getting under each other's skin. Friends that happened to have had a one night stand that was sexy as hell. Just friends.

The ax throwing was set up so two people competed at a time. You stood side by side and threw the ax at a wall that had a big target on it for scoring. Liam and Leah motioned for Grace and I to go first, so we each stepped up to the line on our respective sides. "Ladies first," I said with a wink and watched Grace throw the first ax, which hit the wall sideways and immediately fell to the ground. I tried my best not to laugh, wondering if Grace was going to be super competitive over this.

Grace glared over at me, clearly aware that I found her last attempt humorous. "OK, hot shot. Let's see what you've got."

I lifted the ax over my head and let it go at just the right moment for it to soar perfectly straight and stick right in the center of the bullseye. It was complete luck, but there was no way I was going to admit that. "Turns out, that's what I've got," I boasted.

Grace groaned as she picked her ax up off the ground and walked back to the line to get ready to throw it again. As I watched her arms extend over her head, I could tell this was going to be a dud as well. I cleared my throat to get her attention. "Do you think I could give you some pointers?" Without waiting for an answer, I started walking toward her.

"Listen I don't need your…" Grace's words fell as soon as I wrapped my arms around her from behind. I pushed in much closer than I had to, which immediately brought me back to the club. As much as I truly meant the reasons that I told Grace we should have sex, I had also gotten really turned on dancing with her. I couldn't remember a time in the past when dancing made me that desperate to rip someone's clothes off. I also wouldn't have thought that throwing axes would get me turned on either, but here we were. I slowly moved my hands up Grace's arms, satisfied with the goosebumps I felt forming, that told me this was affecting her just as much as it was affecting me. Once my hands made it onto the ax, I placed them over hers. "Do you trust me?" I whispered. I felt her body shiver against mine as she simply nodded in response.

For a moment, I forgot what we were doing and got lost in the desire pulsing between us. When I finally shook myself free of the hold she had over me, I directed our hands back, then catapulted the ax toward the wall. Clearly we were both too distracted to throw it correctly because it landed outside of the target.

"At least it stuck into the wall that time," Liam yelled from behind us, causing Grace to jump out of my hold. *Freaking men.*

We finished out the last of our throws for that round on our own sides, then Leah took Grace's spot since I had won and got to keep playing. Leah brought the ax above her head to throw it, then brought it back down instead. "Aren't you going to offer to give me a not-so-private ax throwing lesson?" she asked, chuckling at her own joke.

"Ha-Ha," I quipped. "No need to be jealous."

"Oh I'm not jealous. I honestly just thought we might get kicked out. I have a feeling they frown upon people having sex right out in the open here."

"If you think that was sex, then maybe I need to have a little chat with your boyfriend back there. He's clearly doing something wrong." I turned to motion toward Liam in an effort to sneak a peek at whether Grace was listening to our conversation. When I saw the two of them deep in a conversation of their own, I turned back to Leah. "Hey, I can't help it that your childhood friend is smoking hot, and our sexual chemistry is off the charts."

Leah smiled slightly before becoming serious again. "Just please don't hurt her, OK, Kins?"

"You sound like a broken record. I don't know what kind of person you think I am, but I told you that I wouldn't hurt her. I mean that."

"I know. I'm sorry. She just has a tendency to get really attached to people, and even though she claims she won't, I'm afraid that she'll develop feelings, and you'll hurt her without meaning to."

I didn't know what to say in response to that, so I turned back toward my target and took my turn. It turned out that I was an ax throwing expert, so I easily beat Leah and Liam as well. Once I had successfully won every round, I motioned for Grace to come back into the ax throwing area. "Time for the next part of 'Operation Love Sucks.' There's three axes here. I want you to think of three things about Becky that really piss you off, then pretend that you're throwing this ax at her head."

Grace's eyebrows came together, and she tilted her head, the slightest sign of a smile coming to her face. "That seems a bit harsh. How about I pretend it's her hand or something?"

This girl was too much sometimes. "I don't care if you pretend it's her pointer finger. I just want you to throw some damn axes."

"Fine," Grace laughed, pulling the first ax from my hand. "*This* is for cheating on me." As soon as the ax hit the wall with a loud thud, she turned to grab the next one from me. "And *this* is for insisting that you should get to keep our apartment."

She grabbed the last ax from me without even looking to see where that one hit. "AND THIS…" she screamed, getting really worked up with this one, "is for never letting me watch Pretty Little Liars."

When she looked back over at me with a fire in her eyes that I had never seen before, I nodded in response. "Good. Not sure I understand the passion behind that last one, but I'll take it."

Before I knew it, that fire turned into joy, and she excitedly skipped over to me, placing a hand on my shoulder and a light kiss on my cheek. The surprise contact made me freeze up, and Grace quickly jumped back. "Sorry about that. I just got really excited. This has been a very therapeutic process for me."

I did my best to regain my composure. *Get ahold of yourself Kinsley. It was one damn kiss on the cheek. One damn kiss on the cheek that somehow has your head spinning, but still.* "I'm glad to hear that because I'm honestly making this up as I go along," I teased.

Grace relaxed in response to my teasing. "Well, it's working. Also, all of this ax throwing made me hungry. What do you guys say we get some pizza?"

We drove to a pizza shop just a block away, but Leah grabbed me before I could follow Grace and Liam in. "I'm really sorry about what I said earlier. You're a really good person. I've obviously always known that, but I think it's really cool what you're doing for Grace."

I waved a hand. "It's nothing. I'm sure you would have done the same if the timing was different. You know, minus the whole sex thing."

I turned around to go inside, but Leah pulled at my arm again. "I also wanted to tell you to be careful. I don't want you to get hurt either, and I guess I just finally realized that was a possibility."

I scoffed at her concern. "Come on Leah. The only way I could get hurt is if I developed feelings. We both know that's not going to happen."

A look of disbelief came onto Leah's face. "OK. Whatever you say, Kinsley," she answered sarcastically.

This time, I did turn around and head inside. *What the hell was she talking about?* As we all sat eating our pizza, I tried my best to forget about her words. I didn't have feelings. Raging hormones? Obviously. But not feelings. That wouldn't happen. It couldn't happen.

"What do you think Kinsley?" Liam asked, interrupting my thoughts.

I shook myself back into reality and focused across the table at where he was sitting. "What did you say? Sorry. I must have zoned out."

"Leah said that this pizza is better than sex. I wanted to know if you agreed with that statement. You *are* the expert on both. Although, I have to admit, I'm a bit hurt by her conclusion."

Leah shoved him playfully. "Maybe I should rephrase that. This pizza is better than *most* sex. It's not better than sex with you though." They stared at each other lovingly, like she had just paid him the highest compliment in the world.

"And, in your heterosexual opinion, what makes some sex better than other sex? A guy that can last more than five minutes?" I jeered, hoping my question would detract from the love eyes I was currently enduring from across the table.

Luckily, my plan worked, and Leah took her eyes off of Liam so she could roll them at me. "You really need to stop believing all of these straight stereotypes. It's not fair to us heterosexuals," she joked. "But if you must know, it's the love that makes it so great. I never thought I'd say this, but the more you care about someone, the better the sex gets."

I cackled at this response, causing a few other customers to turn and look at our table. "False. The better someone is at sex, the better the sex." There was no way I could actually buy into that. If what she was saying was true, it would mean that... well, it didn't matter. Because it wasn't true.

"So, you truly don't think that it has anything to do with the two people involved? Just the set of skills they possess?" Leah pushed. I looked at Liam and Grace who both seemed uncomfortable with the direction this conversation had taken, but this was the type of relationship Leah and I had. We liked to push the boundaries. Hell, we had no boundaries. I loved this back and forth way too much to drop it for their sake.

"I didn't say that exactly. There can be sexual chemistry. But that's either there or it's not. Feelings will absolutely, 100% not make the sex any better. Sex is sex and that's just how it is."

"Says the girl who has no feelings."

"Whatever," I huffed. "Let's take a poll. Who at this table agrees with me?" When no one raised their hand, I let out an exasperated sigh. "I guess I should have known that would be the case. But I honestly can't believe you guys actually think that's true."

"And I can't believe we're actually talking about this in the middle of a pizza shop," Grace finally spoke.

Liam pointed across the table at her and nodded his head. "I agree. Could we please change the subject?"

I took a big bite of my pizza, then winked. "This pizza *is* really good."

Chapter 12: Grace

A month had passed since I came to Philadelphia, and Leah, Kinsley, and I had fallen into a pretty steady rhythm. Mostly, Leah spent the majority of her time either working or at Liam's, and Kinsley and I spent our time together. As we laid on opposite ends of the couch one Saturday morning watching TV, it hit me that Kinsley had learned a ton about me, but I still knew almost nothing about her. I hit the power button on the TV remote, then laid it back down between us. "You know what? I just realized that I really don't know anything about you. I've told you so much and you've told me nothing."

Kinsley picked the remote up from where I placed it and turned the TV back on. "There's nothing to tell."

Two could play at this game. "Oh come on. I'm not telling you to divulge your deepest, darkest secrets. Just tell me something about your childhood or what you were like in college." *Off.*

"I'd rather not." *On.*

"Seriously?" *Off.*

"Yep." *On.*

"OK. Then tell me more about Lenny." *Off.*

Kinsley picked up the remote again, but then sat it back down. "Fine. But only because he is my favorite topic of conversation, and I also have a feeling that you won't let this drop until I give you *something*. But just for the record, that doesn't mean you won."

I dug my foot into her side. "Oh yeah. Of course not," I mocked.

"Mr. Lenny Lesden Scott entered my life on the 20th of May 2006, when I was a junior in high school. I bought him, but I consider him a rescue because the pet store I got him at was shady and awful. Chinchillas are delicate creatures. They don't bond with just anyone, but if you get them to bond with you, they'll love you for life."

"Delicate creatures?" I cut in. "I take it that's why you and Lenny get along so well."

Kinsley took the pillow she was laying on and tossed it across the couch at me. "This is about Lenny, *not* me. Anyway… Lenny has been my ride or die ever since. For thirteen years, he's always been by my side… or, at least, by my bed. And before you say anything about his age, most chinchillas live between 15 to 20 years. Some can even live 25. So he's not going anywhere, anytime soon."

"I wouldn't have said anything because I already knew that. I'm a big nerd, remember?" I hesitated for a moment, wondering if I should push it by asking my next question, but decided to go for it. "So… where has Lenny lived in his 13 years?"

Luckily, Kinsley smiled at this question. "I see exactly what you're trying to do here, but I also respect the effort, so I'm going to tell you. Lenny started out his life in a wee little town about three hours from here. Then he spent four years in Wisconsin before moving back to wee little town. After another year there, he decided to go to Philadelphia, where he has been ever since."

"Wisconsin, huh? What made you choose to go to school there?"

Upon hearing this question, Kinsley turned the TV back on. I watched her, waiting for an answer, but she just stared at the TV instead. There was something that told me she had so much locked inside that she refused to let out, and I found myself wanting to be the person to extract it from her. "I can feel you staring at me," Kinsley announced, without pulling her eyes from the TV.

"Oh, I wasn't..."

Before I could finish my sentence, Kinsley interrupted. "Listen if you have some strange fascination with finding more out about me, it's gotta be worth it to me. I have an idea, but it will have to wait until later, because if I have to sit around talking about our favorite colors and shit, I want to be drunk."

I snorted in response to Kinsley's ridiculous outlook. "And what is this idea?" I asked, feeling surprisingly just as excited as I was scared.

The smile that entered onto Kinsley's face did nothing to tamper either of those feelings. "I'm tentatively calling it *Truth for a Dare*. That's all I'm telling you for now. I need to go get writing done. Meet me out here at 5:00 with Chinese and booze." Without any further explanation, Kinsley stood up off the couch and walked out of the room.

Several hours later, we were back together on the couch. "So, it's just like it sounds," Kinsley explained. "For every dare that you do, I have to reveal a truth to you. For example, say I dare you to run around the city naked. If you do it, you can then ask me any question, and I have to answer it."

I thought about her proposition. Every part of it sounded like a terrible idea, and I wasn't sure how anything good could come of it. Yet, I couldn't think of anything I wanted to do more. *Who was this girl that I had become?!* "Fine," I conceded. "I'm in, but you can't make every single dare sexual."

Kinsley stuck out her hand to me. "You have a deal, as long as you don't ask me anything about Wisconsin."

The fact that she would include this stipulation made me want to ask a thousand questions, but I reluctantly shook the hand in front of me. "Deal."

"Oh yeah. One more thing," Kinsley spoke through a mouth full of Chinese food. "Since we're going to be drinking anyway, we're totally going to the club after this. I don't know about you, but I could really use a good lay right about now."

The thought of Kinsley having sex with someone other than me, made my heart drop immediately, and for a moment, I thought I might actually start to cry. I'm not sure why I was reacting this way. It's not like I thought Kinsley was suddenly going to go celibate just because she had sex with me. This whole mess started *because* of Kinsley's obsession with sex. Speaking of which, Kinsley was now looking at me with hungry eyes, most likely already thinking about the person she would take home with her. I cleared my throat. "I'm in for the club. As far as the other part goes, I'll have to see where the night takes me."

"Oh, it's going to take you all sorts of places," Kinsley laughed maniacally. "Let me start with something easy." She tapped her chin in mock contemplation. "I dare you to take a shot of my sweet and sour sauce."

I scrunched my nose up at her. "Seriously?"

Kinsley put both hands up in the air. "I don't make the rules. I just enforce them."

"Technically, you do make the rules," I pointed out. Kinsley responded by giving me a look that said she wasn't going to back down, so I reluctantly swallowed the gooey liquid. "Ok. Your turn. What is your favorite color?"

Kinsley chuckled at my reference to her earlier comment. "It's green." She looked up and stared at me for a second that felt more like a lifetime. "Actually, it's exactly the color of your eyes."

I couldn't stop the blush from coming to my face from her compliment, but I wondered if she actually meant it, or if that was just Kinsley trying to avoid anything becoming too serious. I didn't have much time to contemplate it since she immediately looked away and moved on to her next dare. We kept the first few rounds pretty light with Kinsley giving me sleepover type dares and me asking her kindergarten icebreaker questions in return.

"Alright. Time to step it up," Kinsley announced, cracking the knuckles on both of her hands. "I dare you to unfollow Becky on all social media."

I picked my phone up off of the coffee table and noticed that my hand was trembling. Deleting Becky off of social media seemed so *final.* She really wasn't crossing my mind anymore, so her social media presence was the one thing that reminded me of her. If I deleted her, she would eventually be forgotten. And how can that be? How do you let someone go from being your whole world to being nonexistent in your world? If they disappear, does that mean that all of those years of your life just disappear too? I think this was the part of moving on that I still struggled with. Moving on meant letting go, and letting go meant forever.

I took a deep breath, then forced myself to go through every social media platform that I followed her on. *Goodbye Becky.* The feeling of a hand on my shoulder brought me back to reality, and I realized there was a lone tear running down my cheek. When I looked over toward Kinsley, she seemed concerned. "Are you ok?" she asked softly. The sincerity of her tone surprised me. It always confused me when she would transform like this. Her whole demeanor softened and she became a different person, and at this moment, it was causing a kaleidoscope of butterflies to take host in my stomach. Before I could answer, her hand moved from my shoulder up to my cheek, where she used her thumb to wipe away the tear. The delicateness of her touch caused a small gasp to escape from my lips. Kinsley sighed in response and slowly leaned closer to me. When our lips were just an inch apart, her recently closed eyes opened back up, and I noticed a sudden change in her posture. Kinsley sat unmoving, until her lips finally parted.

"Hit me with your best shot," she whispered, before pulling away.

My body was so overwhelmed by whatever had just happened, that it took me a minute to register that she was talking. "Oh, um…" I cleared my throat and tried to force myself back into the mindset of the game. My eyes caught the bottle of vodka that was sitting out on the coffee table. "How would you feel about taking a shot first?"

Kinsley smiled widely at my request. "Now you're speaking my language." She quickly poured a shot for each of us, then held her glass up to mine. "Cheers to what is sure to be an interesting night."

"Cheers!" I repeated, before forcing the drink down my throat and trying to not cough in response to how potent it was. "Ok, your turn," I finally choked out. There were so many questions running through my head that I wanted to ask Kinsley, but I knew if I pushed her too far, she would pull away. "What was little Kinsley like as a child?"

Upon hearing the question, Kinsley chuckled and got a far away look in her eyes. "Exactly what you would expect. I was a little terror. I have a brother who is eight years older than me. From the time I was like five years old, I wanted to do everything he did. I remember one time, he went spelunking with his friends in this cave close to our house, and they had no idea that I followed them there. I ended up going a different direction than them at one point because I thought it was cool that I could make it through the tiny spaces that they couldn't, but ended up getting stuck. Luckily, my brother heard me yelling, but he couldn't get to me. The police department and the fire department had to be called. My parents were pissed, but I didn't care because I thought I was so cool."

I loved watching the way Kinsley's face lit up as she told this story. She always looked good, but there was something special about the way her eyes were sparkling as she spoke. There was an innocence to her that I wasn't used to seeing, but it made her even prettier somehow. "That doesn't surprise me one bit," I smiled. "I bet your parents had their hands full all the time with you."

"Oh they did. I kept them on their toes pretty much all the way up until high school."

"I'm surprised it didn't get worse once you were in high school. I would have thought that you would have been the type to break all of the rules," I joked. My laughter ceased when I realized that the smile had left Kinsley's face. Instead of saying anything in response, she reached for her drink, which was almost completely full, and finished it in a few big gulps. I reached a hand out and placed it gently on her arm. "I'm really sorry if I struck a nerve. I didn't mean to."

Kinsley flashed me a smile, but it didn't reach her eyes, and I could tell it was fake. "You had no way of knowing," she reassured me.

Without thinking, I ran my fingers along Kinsley's arm to try to comfort her. Her eyes followed the path of my hand as it made its way up her arm. I hesitated for a moment, then rested it against her cheek, running one finger along her smooth skin. Kinsley leaned into my touch and sighed softly. In that moment, all I wanted to do was bring my lips to hers. I wanted to kiss her silly until she forgot about everything that had hurt her in the past. I knew that wasn't my place though, so I reluctantly moved my hand and placed it back at my side. I continued to stare over at her, hoping she would look back toward me. "What happened in high school Kinsley?" I asked softly.

She finally looked over at me and, for a moment, she opened her mouth as if she was about to answer me. Just as quickly, she turned back to the coffee table and started to pour herself another drink. "You see. I can't tell you that. Not until you do your next dare," she joked. Though her words were coated in sarcasm, there was still a different tone to her voice than earlier.

"Fine. What is the next dare?"

A sincere smile entered onto Kinsley's face, which had me worried about what was about to come out of her mouth. "OK. Give me a lap dance."

My body immediately reacted in response to her dare. Giving Kinsley a lap dance meant getting up close and personal with her, which is all I had been able to think about since that night two weeks ago. The only issue was that I knew nothing about how to give a lap dance. Heck, I barely knew how to dance. "How about we do another shot first?" I suggested, before I could overthink it.

"Shots and lap dances? Count me in," Kinsley quipped, quickly pouring the drinks.

After forcing it down, I stood up to fulfill my task, realizing as soon as I was on my feet just how much the alcohol had started to affect me. I put a hand on Kinsley's shoulder to steady myself, and she added a hand on my hip for extra support. "This should be very interesting," she laughed, then grabbed her phone and turned on a song that I had never heard before.

I tried my best to get in rhythm with the music, but my dance moves just felt robotic. I turned so my back was facing Kinsley and did a booty shake that was anything but sexy. I remembered watching a movie once where someone gave a lap dance and tried to imitate the moves I saw in that by slowly backing into her. Instead of seductively rubbing up against her, I ended up falling onto her lap. When I tried to stand, I lost my footing and fell back onto her again. I felt Kinsley's body rocking below me and realized it was because she was laughing. I turned to glare at her, and she put her hand over her mouth. "I'm sorry, Grace, but this is by far the most awkward lap dance I have ever gotten." Soon her tiny giggles turned into roaring laughter.

"So, you've had multiple lap dances?" I pouted, although I knew I shouldn't be upset or surprised by this fact.

A cocky grin came onto Kinsley's face. "I've had a few."

This revelation brought on a whole new level of motivation, and I turned around so I was straddling Kinsley's lap. I ran my hands along her legs, then up her sides, feeling my confidence building. "Is this better?" I whispered into her ear, hoping it would sound as seductive as I imagined.

Kinsley swallowed audibly. "I wouldn't exactly call this dancing," she pointed out, but the way her voice trembled as she spoke told me that I was having an effect on her.

"How about now?" I asked, as I ground my hips up against hers. The friction between us sent shockwaves through my whole body, and I suddenly found myself wishing that there weren't so many layers of clothing between us.

"You're definitely making progress," she answered breathlessly. She moved her hands onto my hips and pulled me closer to her. Soon, she was leaning into me and kissing my neck, just like she had the night we had sex. With that move, I had officially lost control of my body and was ready for her to do whatever she wanted to me. Her mouth moved up to my ear, and her breath made me shiver. "How would you feel about a quickie before the club?"

And just like that, the moment was gone. Leave it to Kinsley to completely ruin it. I pulled myself off of her and sat back down on the couch, making sure to leave space between us. Kinsley wanted a quickie before going to the club. The club where she was planning to find someone else to have sex with. "Is that seriously all I mean to you?" I asked, exasperated.

"Oh come on. It was a joke," Kinsley fought back. I gave her a look that told her that I didn't find it funny, and she softened a bit. "I'm sorry, OK? I make stupid jokes when I get nervous, and for whatever reason, you in all your awkward glory make me really nervous sometimes."

"And why is that?" I asked, desperate to know what she was thinking for once.

Kinsley lifted one eyebrow at me. "Is this your truth question? Because if it is, this is all you get. Don't think I'm going to answer this *and* tell you anything about high school."

I nodded for her to go on, frustrated that she insisted on continuing to play this stupid game. "OK then," Kinsley sighed. "The truth is, I honestly don't know. All I know is that you make me feel things that I can't quite explain, and I can't decide if I love it or I hate it, and that makes me nervous."

I wanted to tell Kinsley that I completely understood because I felt the exact same way. She made me feel more than I had felt in a really long time. I didn't know if it was lust or something else, but I also wasn't sure if it really made any difference when it came to Kinsley. "And what do you want me to do with that information?" I asked nervously.

Kinsley shook her head. "Absolutely nothing. I want you to forget I even said it." *Typical.* "Get ready to go to the club, and then I'll let you know what your next dare is."

I wanted to fight her and tell her that I was done with this game, but instead I headed to Leah's room to get ready. A half hour later, I joined her back in the living room of the apartment. Kinsley was wearing a tight leather skirt with a white t-shirt tucked into it. She had curled her hair for a change, and I had to remind myself not to drool. She looked good. Really good. Too good, actually. Kinsley, not-so-subtly, ran her eyes over my outfit, which was nowhere near as sexy as hers. When she caught me watching her, she winked at me. "This next dare should be no problem for you at all."

"Do I even want to know what it is?" I groaned.

"Maybe. Maybe not," she laughed. "But you don't have a choice. You are going to make out with some rando at the club tonight, and in return, I'll tell you all of my woe-is-me stories from high school."

"Fine," I agreed. I didn't particularly want to make out with someone in the club. Even with the steady buzz I had going, it wasn't my style. If I was going to be making out with someone tonight, I only wanted it to be one person in particular, but this person was currently suggesting I find someone else, which only further proved that Kinsley didn't actually feel the same way. I prayed that kissing someone else would break whatever hold it was that Kinsley suddenly had over me.

Chapter 13: Kinsley

We had only been in the club for ten minutes, and Grace was already actively searching for the person she would ultimately attempt to seduce. Although, I had a feeling it wasn't going to be too hard for her. Grace looked sexy as hell. She was wearing a green dress that fell just above her knees and had on green glasses to match. The green from the glasses caused her eyes to look even more spectacular than usual. Seeing her walk out into the living room had literally taken my breath away, and it took everything in me not to suggest that we just stay back at the apartment and have some fun of our own. I had a feeling Grace wasn't going to go for that though, especially after how mad my quickie comment had made her. I didn't even know why I had said that. The last thing I wanted in that moment was a quickie, which is probably exactly *why* I said it. The way my body reacted to Grace wasn't normal, and I needed to shake that feeling.

The sound of laughter brought me back to the present moment, and I soon realized that it was Grace reacting to something that a very pretty brunette was whispering in her ear. The pretty brunette turned toward me when she caught me staring. "I hope you don't mind, but I'm going to steal your friend for a bit," she informed me.

I wiggled my eyebrows and gave them both a thumbs up as they stumbled onto the dance floor together. My eyes remained glued to them as they began to dance close. I couldn't tear my eyes away from the two of them. I mean, I *had* to watch. I needed proof that Grace went through with her dare. I couldn't just take her word for it. Then the moment came. The pretty brunette leaned in close and captured Grace's lips with her own. I watched to see how Grace would respond, and my stomach dropped when she passionately continued what the brunette had started. I tore my eyes away from the scene. It hurt to watch, which didn't make sense. This was my idea. It was my dare. I should have been happy that Grace was breaking out of her shell. This is what we had been working toward. In that moment though, I felt anything but happiness. I turned back toward the bar so I could motion for the bartender to bring me another drink. I was interrupted by the feeling of a tap on my shoulder. I didn't want to turn around though. I wasn't in the mood to talk to anyone. The person refused to give up, grabbing my shoulder to force me to turn around. When I finally gave in, it was Grace's big green eyes that I was staring into. Her eyes scanned the length of my face, stopping for a moment on my lips, before looking back into mine. She swallowed hard before speaking. "Now that I did my dare, it's time for me to ask you a question."

I only nodded in response since I couldn't seem to find my words at that moment. Grace continued to silently stare at me for what felt like an eternity. "I was just wondering if…" she paused, as if she was starting to rethink what she was about to say, but then sighed in defeat. "I was wondering if you wanted to kiss me as badly as I want to kiss you right now. Because the whole time I was kissing her, the only thing I could think about was how much I wanted it to be you and I just…"

Before Grace could finish, I crashed my lips into hers. She immediately wrapped her arms around my neck and pulled me closer to her. My hands instinctively went to her hips as the kiss deepened. Our bodies were so close that it felt like they had meshed into one, and for a moment, I forgot we were standing in the middle of the club. When the sounds of music hit my ears, I pulled back. The desire I saw in

Grace's eyes matched what I was feeling, so I figured it was safe to use my next line. "I dare you to come home with me."

"I kind of live with you right now, so I don't really have a choice," Grace answered innocently.

I rolled my eyes at her and placed another chaste kiss on her lips. "Shut up. You know exactly what I mean. But I'll beg if I have to." I put both of my hands up in a praying motion. "Grace, will you pretty pretty please have sex with me?"

The smile that was already adorning Grace's face, grew exponentially with my words. "I thought you'd never ask."

That was all I needed to hear. I picked her up and carried her out of the club, putting her down only so we could make it back to the apartment more quickly. I didn't even bother to call for a ride. There was no need for foreplay right now. I was happy to find the apartment pitch black, indicating that Leah decided not to come home for the night. As soon as we were in my room, Grace's hands were on the zipper of my skirt. "I'm sorry, but I need you right now," she pleaded.

I was just happy we were on the same page, and before I knew it, we were both lying on my bed naked, gasping for air. Even though it hadn't taken us very long to make it to this point, I certainly wouldn't have called it a quickie. It was so much more than that. "So, why Laurel Lake?" Grace questioned, once she was able to catch her breath.

I was surprised by the question, expecting her to go back to our earlier conversation about high school. I turned onto my side so I was facing her, and she did the same. "Laurel is my middle name, and I grew up on Hidden Lake Road."

"Kinsley Laurel Scott. That's a very pretty name." Grace put one hand on my cheek, then placed a gentle kiss on my lips that made me want to roll on top of her and have my way with her all over again. "It's fitting for you. A beautiful name for a beautiful girl."

I giggled at her cheesiness. "That's so lame… in the most adorable way possible of course." Before our silence overtook the room, I spoke up again. "Laurel was also my grandma's name. She was my best friend, but she died at the end of my sophomore year in college. And to answer your question - *no,* I don't want to talk about it."

"I won't force you to talk about anything you don't want to," Grace reassured me, but something about the sincerity in her voice made me want to tell her everything. "Do you want to tell me what happened in high school? It's OK if you don't."

"It's really no big deal," I answered as nonchalantly as possible. "It's the typical gay kid in a small town story. I started to realize I was gay around the end of junior high, and it scared the crap out of me. Growing up, gay was a derogatory term that people used to insult each other. We had full sermons in church about the dangers of homosexuality. If there was someone in town who people suspected was gay, the gossip and rumors would start flying. My own parents told me I should walk a different way to school when they heard that one of our neighbors might be gay. It was like they automatically assumed that his sexual preference made him some sort of pedophile or criminal. So, I retreated. I spent most of my time on the internet, escaping to places where I could be myself. I had no interest in going to a barn and getting drunk with a bunch of people who were just going to question why I wasn't actively on the hunt for my future husband. That's also why I became so close to my grandma. We were always pretty close, but I started spending all of my time, that wasn't spent lost in the World Wide Web of lesbians, with her. We would play cards or watch scary movies or just talk. She was the one person in my life who didn't insist on talking about my dating life or my plans for the future. Sometimes I wonder if she realized I was gay, and that's why she never pushed that stuff. I guess I'll never know." I looked over at Grace, who had her eyes focused intently on me, as if she was soaking up every single word. I had become so caught up in my story that I honestly forgot I was saying it out loud. "Bet you're surprised to hear that Kinsley Scott used to spend Friday nights playing rummy with her grandma. Probably takes away some of the allure, huh?" I joked, trying to break the tension in the room.

Grace put her arms around me to pull me closer, then nuzzled her head into my neck, placing kisses where her lips met my skin. The sensation of her naked body against mine along with the kisses was almost too much to handle. "Quite the opposite actually," she spoke into my neck. "Seeing this side of you just makes me more turned on and ready for round two."

I pulled back so Grace could see my face, then flashed her my sexiest half smile. "That could be arranged," I teased while wiggling my eyebrows and attempting to crawl on top of her.

Much to my dismay, Grace put her hand up to stop me. "As much as I would enjoy that, I'm not going to jump your bones immediately after you confessed that to me. I would feel like I was taking advantage of you."

"Just for the record, I'm very OK with you taking advantage of me anytime," I pointed out, attempting my quest one more time, only to be denied again. I groaned as I rolled away, but Grace pulled me back.

"I'm really sorry that you went through that," she cooed, as she ran a hand through my hair. "I get the whole small town thing, but I was so far in the closet when I was in high school that even I didn't realize I was gay, so I wouldn't know what that feels like. Sure, my town still has a few bigots, but for the most part people have changed with the times. It's strange to imagine you that way though. I would have thought you would have been all *take me or leave me.*"

Her words made me laugh. "I became that way eventually, but it just took me awhile."

"And is that why you went all the way to Wisconsin for college?" Grace asked hesitantly.

"Something like that," I shrugged. Grace may have had a way of getting me to open up, but there was no way she was going to get all of those details.

Grace's hand moved from my hair, onto my back, where she lightly ran her nails across my skin. "I know that was all really hard for you to talk about, and I want you to know that I appreciate you opening up to me. What can I do for you right now?"

This was normally the point when I would make some lewd comment and insist that we go for that round two she mentioned, but that surprisingly wasn't what I wanted. "Could you… could you just hold me?" I realized that I sounded like a small child who had just woken up from a nightmare, but I couldn't bring myself to care. The smile on Grace's face made all of my reservations fade away. In that moment, I wanted nothing more than to fall into the arms that were outstretched for me, so that's exactly what I did.

When I awoke, three hours later, initially frightened by the other body in bed with me, the moment was gone. I groaned as I remembered the events that had occurred a few hours earlier. How had I let this happen?! Not the sex. The sex was great. Sure, it always ran the risk of complicating things when a one-time thing became more than that. But that wasn't what had me freaking out. I wasn't the type of person to have deep conversations following sex, and I certainly wasn't someone who cuddled. That broke every rule I had ever established for myself. I didn't know how I had let Grace have this effect on me, but it needed to stop.

I slipped out of bed, being careful not to wake her and made myself comfortable on the couch. It seemed like I had just fallen back asleep when I felt a tap on my shoulder. I blinked up to see Leah staring down at me. "Why are you sleeping on the couch?" She looked at the blanket that was only partially covering me, then started to laugh. "Are you naked?"

I was about to ask her what she was doing home so early, when I heard my bedroom door open and Grace's voice calling from the hallway. "Kinsley? Is everything OK? You weren't in bed, and I didn't..."

Grace stopped dead in her tracks when she noticed Leah standing by the couch. Luckily, she was clothed, but there wasn't much of a secret about what had happened given that she was standing there wearing her dress from the night before and had guilt plastered across her face. Leah looked back and forth between the two of us and shook her head playfully. "How long have you guys been continuing to have sex behind my back?"

"Oh, we haven't," Grace quickly spoke. "It just sort of... happened again... last night."

"Yeah, we were pretty tanked," I added.

"Soooooo, what does this mean?" Leah asked excitedly.

"It means nothing," I scoffed. I felt guilty about my choice of words, so I added, "Sorry. What I meant to say is that it just means that we are two friends who happen to be very compatible in the bedroom. Nothing more than that."

Leah rolled her eyes at me, then turned to Grace, who nodded in confirmation. "Whatever you say. How about the three of us *buddies* do something fun today?"

I stood from the couch and wrapped the blanket around my naked body. "I think you two should just have some bestie time today. I need to get some writing done anyway. Have fun though." Before anyone could say anything else, I zipped through the hall and into my bedroom, shutting the door behind me.

After about two hours of staring at a blank computer screen, I heard a knock on my door. When I opened it, I found Grace standing on the other side. She was wearing jean shorts and a plain, red t-shirt and had her hair pulled up in a messy ponytail, but still looked stunning. It took everything in me not to pull her into my room and start kissing her. "I just wanted to let you know that we are going for a walk through the city and possibly hitting up a few bars. Are you sure you don't want to come?"

"I really *do* need to get work done. I have a bunch of deadlines coming up," I lied.

Grace tilted her head and studied my face as if she wasn't buying a word I was saying. "Are we ok? You know... after everything that happened last night."

I scoffed in an attempt to feign nonchalance. "Of course we are. We're two mature adults. We don't have to get all weird just because we had sex again."

Grace nodded, then went to turn around. She looked like she was about to walk away when she looked back at me again. "Just so you know, I'm not expecting anything to change after last night. I realize I'm not the type who normally does casual, but you don't have to pull away from me to prove a point. I understand that we're just friends. I don't think either of us are looking for more than that."

"Obviously. It was just sex."

"Exactly. Just sex," Grace repeated more softly, before shutting my door and leaving me alone with my thoughts once again.

I wasn't trying to pull away from Grace. I just needed some space while whatever was going on inside of me simmered down a bit. That was it. Then things could go back to normal, whatever that was when Grace was involved.

***

As the week passed, I found any excuse I could to avoid spending time together. It was working pretty well, aside from the fact that I missed her terribly, which was strange since she had the tendency to drive me insane when we were together. By the end of the week, Grace seemed to have gotten the point and stopped making an effort to pull me out of my room. When I heard a knock on my door Thursday night, I started running through a list of excuses in my head. Before I could stand from my desk, the door swung open. "Hey stranger!" Leah shouted at me. "How is it going hiding out in your room?"

I glared at her in response to her question. "I'm not hiding out. I just have a lot of work to get done, ok? I want to get this book published by the end of the summer and also have a few freelance article deadlines coming up."

"Oh, OK. So, this has nothing to do with that sexy redhead that you decided to hook up with again last weekend?" Just the thought of Grace and our last time together made my whole body feel like it was on fire. *So much for simmering down.*

"That sexy redhead has a name, you know. You should learn to be more respectful of women," I jeered. "But, as a matter of fact, no - it has nothing to do with Grace. We are just fine."

Leah lifted an eyebrow at me. "Whatever you say. We just ordered pizza, so you have about 45 more minutes to hide out, and then you have to come join us."

"I'll sit this one out. We have pizza all the time."

"Yeah, because it's your favorite food. You've told me countless times that you would live off of pizza and Chinese food if it was socially acceptable, so don't pull that lame excuse with me."

I rolled my eyes. "Fine. I'll be out once I hear the doorbell." And that's exactly what I did. I waited until the exact moment that the pizza arrived and then joined Grace, Liam, and Leah out in the living room.

"How's work going?" Grace asked as soon as I sat down. *This girl and all of her damn questions all the time.*

"Work is fine. It's work. Any other questions or can I enjoy my pizza?"

Grace's face immediately turned red, and for a moment, I felt bad for giving her attitude. "Nope. No questions at all, Kinsley. Forget I even asked. Sorry for caring," she snapped.

"I never asked you to care, so that's your own problem," I laughed.

Before I could evaluate Grace's reaction, Leah cleared her throat on the other side of me. "So, Liam and I had an idea."

"Actually, it was your ide…." Liam began, but Leah put a hand up to stop him.

"*Liam* and I had an idea. We think that the four of us should go camping this weekend."

"The four of us? Is that like a *thing* now?" I mocked.

Leah made a face at me in response to my joke, and I couldn't tell whether it was amusement, annoyance, or a little bit of both. "OK, Kins. Two things." She held up two fingers to make a point. "One… I'm going to need you to stop being a big old bag of douche. And two… for this weekend, the four of us are a *'thing'* and we are all going camping whether you like it or not."

Grace looked between Leah and I, then hesitantly spoke up. "I'm not sure if…"

"I said….the four of us are going camping this weekend whether you like it or not," Leah interrupted.

Grace and I reluctantly agreed. We both knew Leah well enough to know that once she made up her mind about something, there was no turning back, which was exactly how I found myself crawling into the back of Liam's Jeep not even 24 hours later.

"Any music requests?" Liam asked once we were on the road.

At the exact same time that I said, "EDM," Grace answered with, "Something relaxing."

Liam and Leah gave each other a look, at which point Leah turned on the radio. "Top 40 it is."

The four of us were mostly quiet as we drove the rest of the way to the campsite. Once we arrived, Liam started pulling supplies out of the back of the car. "So, where's the third tent?" I asked, after only seeing two in the pile.

"Liam only has two tents," Leah answered nonchalantly. "Since you and Grace have shared a bed a few times, I figured you'd be fine sharing a tent."

"Sounds great," I responded through gritted teeth.

Since we had arrived late, we decided to spend a few hours around a campfire before going to bed. I volunteered to start it even though I had no clue what I was doing. Camping really wasn't my thing, but I just wanted some time away from the group. Unfortunately, that time didn't last too long. As soon as Grace noticed me struggling, she joined me by the fire pit. "Could I help you?"

"I'm fine," I snapped. "I got this." I continued to rub sticks together the way I had seen it done in movies.

"I just think there's an easier…"

"I don't care what you think. I said that I've got this."

As I continued to struggle, Grace reached for something in her pocket. I didn't notice that it was a lighter until she had the whole pile of leaves and branches in front of me up in flames. A cocky smile came onto her face as she put the lighter back in her pocket. "You're welcome."

"I didn't say thank you," I growled.

Grace slammed her fist on the ground, then quickly stood up. "You know what Kinsley?! Maybe you wouldn't be so freaking miserable all the time if you actually let people in." Before I could respond, she stormed back to our tent, zipping it up fully once she was inside.

Leah watched the scene, then walked up to me with both hands in the air. "What the heck just happened?"

"Same old, same old," I replied. "Turns out, if we're not bumping vaginas, we're butting heads."

Leah mockingly gagged. "Ew. I'm going to pretend you didn't just put that visual in my head. You do realize why you guys fight all the time though, right?"

"Because she takes things too personally, and I'm kind of an asshole?"

"Well, this is true. But there's also the fact that you both have feelings that you're trying to suppress. You want to fight those feelings so badly that you're fighting each other instead."

"That's ridiculous," I fought, joining Liam who was now sitting by the fire.

Liam looked between Leah and I. "What happened to Grace?"

Leah pointed one thumb toward me. "Asshole over here struck again and did something to upset her."

To my surprise, Liam started to laugh and shake his head. "You guys really need to just admit that you have feelings for each other."

Really? Liam too? What had Leah been saying to him? The last thing I wanted was to deal with people trying to tell me how I felt, so I stood back up. "You guys have fun. I'm just going to go to bed too."

As I walked away, Leah began to snicker. "Make sure you guys keep the noise down during the make up sex. We don't want to scare the wildlife."

I shook my head at her. Of course there wouldn't be any make up sex. There wouldn't be any more sex period. It didn't matter how good it was or how much I wanted it. It couldn't happen. Clearly, Grace was getting the wrong idea, and I wasn't going to let it continue.

At least, that's what I told myself. As soon as I was in the tent, staring at Grace's sleeping form, all of my previous convictions went out the window. If Grace would wake up and ask to have sex with me, I'd be naked in about a half a second. I found her aggravatingly irresistible. I scolded myself for letting her have this effect on me, as I changed into pajamas and crawled into my sleeping bag. The tent was way too small for two people who were trying not to touch, so I could feel every movement Grace was making in the sleeping bag next to me. Soon, I realized she was shaking.

I put a hand on her bare shoulder and tried to ignore how my stupid heartbeat picked up from this one simple touch. "Are you OK?" I whispered.

"I'm fine." Grace's words were short. She was clearly still annoyed from earlier. After a few beats, she sighed in defeat. "I'm just freezing. I didn't pack any warm clothes. I totally didn't think about the fact that it would cool down so much once the sun went down."

I scooted my sleeping bag even closer to hers. "I know one way we could warm ourselves up real quickly," I breathed into her neck and was happy when I saw goosebumps form in response.

Grace was still for a minute, then turned to look at me. Unfortunately, she gave me a look of annoyance rather than desire. "Seriously, Kinsley? You can't just treat me however you want and then expect that I'll have sex with you again. You ignored me all week, and whenever you did talk to me, you were a jerk."

"It was just sex, Grace. I never claimed that I was going to ride into the sunset with you."

"And who says that's what I want?" Her question took me aback. I wasn't expecting that response, and for whatever reason, I didn't like hearing it. *But why would that bother me? It's good that she doesn't have any expectations. I don't want expectations. I hate expectations.*

"If I had to guess, I'd say your Laurel Lake fan page probably does," I attempted to joke.

Unfortunately, as usual with Grace, my joke fell flat. She rolled her eyes and quickly turned away from me. "Goodnight Kinsley," she mumbled.

As I laid there contemplating why I seemed to get under her skin so much, I noticed she was still shivering. I reached out a hand and placed it on her arm. Even with the way my hand seemed to burn from the contact with her skin, I could still tell that she was freezing. I moved closer and wrapped my arms around her from behind. I could tell by the way that her body stiffened at my touch that she was still awake. "I'm sorry about my joke," I whispered into her ear. "Please let me hold you. I want to help warm you up."

I couldn't believe these words were leaving my mouth. Who had I become around this girl? But then again, I wasn't going to just let someone die of hypothermia. Not when I had plenty of body heat to provide. I would do this for anyone. The fact that she was a pretty girl just made it more enjoyable. Grace simply nodded in response, and I crawled into her sleeping bag with her, easily slipping into a deep sleep.

I awoke the next day to the sound of Leah and Liam talking outside of our tent. I opened my eyes to see Grace still snuggled up against me and thought about prolonging this moment as long as I could. But why would I do that when I could spend the day outside? I *really* had to shake this feeling, but first I had to shake myself loose from the girl I strangely had no interest in leaving. I carefully extracted myself, careful not to wake her, then headed outside. "Hey! How is my favorite grumpy pants today?" Leah teased as soon as she saw me.

"Ha very funny," I mocked. "What's the plan for today?"

Liam held up his fishing rod in one hand and a can of beer in the other. "Welp, I already caught our fish for dinner. I thought the rest of the day could be spent drinking and swimming."

"You woke up super early to fish, *and* you're already drinking? I can't handle you early risers."

Liam scratched at his head and looked down at his watch. "I mean I woke up at 10:30, so I wouldn't exactly call that early. I guess someone who wakes up at two might have different ideas though."

I grabbed his wrist to look at his watch and was shocked to see that he wasn't lying. I don't know if I had ever slept that well. Must have been something about the great outdoors.

Within a half hour, Grace was awake, and we were already down at the lake swimming and drinking. Leah and I sat on the edge, while Grace and Liam jumped right in and began messing around like a bunch of kids. I watched in envy as Liam fought to dunk Grace, wishing it was my hands that were touching that barely covered body.

"Aren't you jealous that your boyfriend has his hands all over some other girl?"

Leah chuckled at my words. "He's far from being all over her, plus she's not just *some other girl.* She's my childhood best friend who is also a big lesbian. Also, even if he was all over her, I wouldn't care. I'm not the jealous type." She looked over at me as I continued to watch them intently. "I guess the same can't be said for you though," she laughed.

"Why would I be jealous of your boyfriend getting handsy with some other girl? In case you missed it, he's not my type."

Leah rolled her eyes at me. "Clearly I'm talking about the fact that you are jealous that someone else is enjoying time with your lady right now."

I jumped in the lake and joined Liam and Grace in order to avoid acknowledging her nonsense. The rest of the day was filled with chicken fights, rope swinging, and lots of drinking. By the time we were done eating dinner, we all had a pretty good buzz going. "I can't decide if I want to throw up or have a bunch of sex with my boyfriend, but either way, I'm going back to the tent, and I suggest *you* should come with me," Leah slurred, while pointing to Liam.

Liam stood and wiggled his eyebrows at Grace and I. "There's a 50% chance that this is going to turn out really well for me, so I'll see you ladies tomorrow."

I turned to Grace who had started to shiver. "Maybe we should call it a night too," I suggested. "You look like you could use your sleeping bag now that the fire has died down." I reached a hand out, and Grace graciously accepted it. We continued to hold hands as we stumbled over to our tent. This time, I automatically crawled into Grace's sleeping bag with her, immediately pulling her into a tight embrace from behind. I was almost asleep when I heard soft whimper come from Grace's direction. "Hey now. What's wrong?" I whispered into her ear, while pulling her even closer to me.

"Sorry, it's really stupid. I wouldn't be crying if I wasn't drunk right now."

I ran my fingers up and down Grace's arm. "Shhh... It's OK. You can tell me."

Grace took a few quick breaths, and I could tell she was trying to fight the tears. "It's just… you're holding me, and the last person who held me like this was Becky, and it just brought back a bunch of memories, and I started thinking about how much I miss having someone that cares about me snuggle up to me every night."

I forced Grace to turn and look at me, then ran a finger along her cheek. As I stared into her green eyes, a slew of emotions rushed through me, and all I wanted to do was make her feel better. "It's going to be OK. You're going to be OK," I soothed. Without thinking, I leaned down and connected my lips with Grace's, then continued to kiss down her chin and neck. Grace sighed and lifted her neck to allow me access. I delicately placed kisses along every square inch, then moved back to her lips, every cell in my body on high alert from this simple contact.

Grace gently pushed me away. "I'm not in the right place to have sex tonight, Kinsley."

I moved a stray hair behind Grace's ear and looked back into her eyes. "I don't need to have sex with you. I just want you to know that I *do* care about you. It might not be in the same way Becky did, but at least that means I can't hurt you. Just trust me when I tell you that you are being held by someone who cares about you."

With this confession, Grace wrapped her arms around my neck and pulled me back into her. The kiss was tentative at first, but soon her tongue was gliding along my bottom lip, begging for entry. I opened my mouth to hers and moaned as our tongues wrapped around each other. The kiss was slow and sensual and remained this way for hours, until we were both too tired to continue and fell asleep in each other's arms.

I was disappointed when I awoke the next day, and Grace was no longer there beside me. The events from the night before replayed in my head, and for once, I didn't regret them. I was starting to realize that this was just the type of friendship that Grace and I had. It was fun, and real, and hot as hell. I moved toward the front of the tent and was about to unzip it when I heard Leah and Liam playfully teasing Grace. I couldn't hear what they were saying, but I figured it probably had something to do with me, so I put my ear against the front of the tent to listen. Grace's voice was the first that I heard. "Alright guys. Drop it. Kinsley and I are just friends. That's all we're ever going to be. I mean, come on Leah. You met Becky. Clearly Kinsley isn't my type."

Her words made me feel like I had just been punched in the gut. I couldn't remember the last time I felt like this. Actually, I could, but it had been years, and I had vowed that I wouldn't let myself feel like this ever again. Luckily, it wasn't too late this time. It wasn't like I had actually fallen for her. I sat in the tent for a few more minutes, before throwing on a t-shirt, shorts, and sneakers.

"Going for a morning jog," I announced as soon as I left the tent.

Grace looked over at me, and a smile lit up her face. "That's a great idea. Just let me get changed, and I'll come with you."

"Did I say you could come?" I snapped. "We don't have to do everything together, Grace."

Before she could respond, I took off jogging in the opposite direction. I had never been much of a runner. Track had been one of the many sports that I quit after less than a year. Even though I was competitive, I couldn't commit to anything, even intramurals. But today, running felt good. It felt liberating. I hadn't been running too long when I came upon a camper with a big rainbow flag on the front. A girl wearing just a pair of daisy duke style shorts and a red bikini top was sitting outside reading. Her long blonde hair was blowing in the slight breeze, and when she looked up from her book, her stunning blue eyes caught me. The smile that came across her face told me that she also liked what she was seeing. I pointed behind her. "Nice flag."

She looked toward the flag and smiled. "We call this thing Ol' Gay."

"We, as in you and your girlfriend?" I teased.

The blonde shook her head slowly. "We, as in me and my friends. Unfortunately, I'm still single."

"I don't see anything unfortunate about that," I flirted back.

An even wider smile spread across the blonde's face as she stood up and reached out a hand toward me. "I'm Serena. It's nice to meet you…"

"Kinsley," I finished, taking her hand in mine. "So, Serena, this may be way too forward of me, but how would you feel about spending some time at my campsite today? That is, unless you think your friends will miss you too much."

Serena looked toward the camper and sighed. "Turns out they're all coupled up at this point, so I'd say they won't miss me one bit. Let me just grab a t-shirt."

"T-shirts aren't required." I ran my eyes the length of her body, showing my appreciation. And what a nice body it was. Sure, my own body didn't react the way it did when I looked at Grace, but that was a good thing.

The two of us talked and flirted as we walked the rest of the way back to my campsite. Once we arrived, three sets of eyes were immediately drawn to my new friend. I put an arm around her waist and smiled proudly. "This is Serena. She's going to spend the day with us."

My friends' greetings were cordial, but forced. Grace looked toward the ground, refusing to make eye contact with me. She seemed upset by my actions, but I wasn't sure why she would be. I wasn't her type after all. There were only four chairs set up outside our tents so I sat down in the remaining one and pulled Serena onto my lap, happy to see that she wasn't shy at all. "So, what's the plan for today?" I asked, looking past the girl on my lap.

Leah looked from me to Grace, who was still staring down at the ground. "Well, I thought the four of us were going to do something today. No offense, Serena."

"Yeah. The four of us are just kind of a thing," Liam added.

Serena looked between all of us, then awkwardly stood from my lap. "Sorry to intrude. It was really nice to meet all of you." Before I could say anything, she was walking away.

"Seriously guys?" I growled. "Way to be a cock block."

Leah only glared at me in response. "Just because you're a dick doesn't mean you have one. Therefore, it can't be considered a *cock* block."

Normally, I would have found this one-liner humorous, but not after the way they had just treated a girl that could have been a very good time for me. And for what reason? It's not like I was tied down. Why shouldn't I be allowed to have a little fun? "Whatever Leah. You three have your thing today. Count me out of it."

I walked away from the campsite without saying another word and headed down toward the lake. Once I was there, I began skipping rocks into the water. Well, if you could call it that. I was more so just chucking them in order to get out all of my frustration. My throws were interrupted by someone putting a hand on my shoulder. I whipped around to see Grace staring at me with those big green eyes; big green eyes that looked extremely sad at the moment. I hated to see her like this, but what I hated even more was the fact that I cared.

"What's going on, Kinsley?" Grace asked softly.

"What's going on?! I was just trying to have a good time, and all of my so-called friends decided to keep that from happening."

"I'm sorry about that," Grace apologized. "I think Liam and Leah were just trying to look out for me."

"Look out for you?!" I snarled. "What?! They need to protect you from mean old Kinsley? Reality check, Grace. We're *not* together. Having amazing sex and snuggling up in a tent doesn't suddenly make us a couple."

Grace's eyes became more sad the longer I spoke, but I forced myself not to care. She looked at the ground and kicked around a rock, before looking back at me. "I never said we were together Kinsley. I know where we stand. That's not what either of us are looking for."

"Exactly. I don't want to get tied down, and you are still stuck on that goddamn ex of yours and, at this point, you probably always will be. It's pathetic."

The sadness drained from Grace's face and was instantly replaced by anger. I didn't know that it was actually possible for someone to turn that shade of red, but Grace was pulling it off beautifully. "Seriously Kinsley?! I don't even know what to say to you anymore. God! Why are you *such* an asshole?!"

I wanted to fight back and tell her that I wasn't an asshole, but that would be a lie. Every single thing I had done so far today would qualify me as an asshole, and I knew Grace didn't deserve it, especially not that last comment. I was too fired up at this point to apologize though. "Do you want to know why I'm an asshole? Do you really want to know?!" I yelled.

"Yes Kinsley! Tell me. Tell me this big secret as to why you choose to be such a jerk when I know that deep down you're one of the nicest, most caring people in this world." Even though her words were complimentary, her tone was still laced in anger.

My emotions continued to build, and I couldn't believe that the words I was about to say were actually going to leave my mouth, but I also knew that I couldn't stop them at this point. "Fine!" I screamed. "I'll tell you. I'm an asshole because I had my heart broken. No, correction, shattered. I'm a freaking cliche, Grace. I hate love because I can't deal with the fact that I once had it and lost it and almost lost my goddamn mind because of it. Being an asshole is my way of pushing people away to make sure that never happens again. I can say whatever I want about you, but I'm still letting a relationship affect me that ended over 9 years ago. Who is the pathetic one now?!" Before I could stop them, tears were running down my face. God, I really hated Grace for having this effect on me.

Grace reached out and put a hand on my arm, which I promptly pulled away. "Kinsley, I'm so…"

I turned away from her. "Stop. Please, Grace. Just leave me alone." When she refused to move, I turned back toward her. "Seriously, go! I don't want to talk to you right now."

I was happy to see that this time Grace obeyed my commands. I needed to be alone at this time. No one should have to deal with this. I didn't even want to deal with this.

Chapter 14: Grace

Almost a week had passed since Kinsley's breakdown on our camping trip, and she had yet to talk to me. It wasn't from lack of trying on my part. Each day, I knocked on her door, asking for her to come out and was met with the same voice telling me to give her space. I was still pissed about how she had treated me on our trip, but at this point, I was more worried than I was mad. I had a feeling that Kinsley hadn't ever opened up to anyone about her breakup, or even her relationship for that matter. Leah and I had spent a lot of time together the past week and from talking to her, I had deduced that she knew nothing about Kinsley's emotional confession. Of course, I didn't share it with her. That was Kinsley's story to share if she ever chose to. Everytime we hung out, Leah stressed that I should give Kinsley time and space, but not hold it against her. Kinsley and Leah had quickly made up after she returned to the campsite later in the afternoon, and Kinsley had actually agreed to go to dinner with her a few nights later. Leah was still insistent upon the fact that Kinsley was such a jerk to me because she had feelings for me, but I wasn't sure if I agreed with that. I thought the whole "she's mean because she likes you" thing died in kindergarten. What did it matter anyway? I was still a mess from my relationship with Becky, and Kinsley had a world of problems of her own. Plus, I wasn't fully convinced that I had feelings for her. Sure, I could barely handle the thought of her close to me without becoming ridiculously turned on, but it wasn't just about the sex. The way it felt when she held me in her arms was indescribable. I never remembered feeling that safe in Becky's arms, even before she started cheating on me. It felt like I belonged there. Like I was made for that space between her arms. When we were molded together like that, the analogy about people being two puzzle pieces made perfect sense to me. Even with my hopeless romantic heart, I could never wrap my head around that idea, until now. Still, she was crude and closed off and almost never took life seriously.

My thoughts were interrupted by a knock on my door. I found it strange that Leah would be knocking when this was technically her room, and she had told me she was leaving for Liam's at least an hour ago, but I didn't know who else it would be. It's not like it was going to be… "Kinsley." My voice shook when I saw it was her standing on the other side of my doorway.

She held up a tiny bag that looked to have some sort of treat inside. "I was just wondering if you wanted to give Lenny his bedtime cookie. Spoiler alert. It's not actually a cookie, but don't tell him that. It's actually just a bunch of herbs and really good for his digestive system. He also should get a bath tonight, so you can watch that too if you want. I'm sure you already know this, but chinchillas don't bathe in water - they bathe in dust." I recognized this rambling. This was the same type of rambling that Kinsley did when we were about to have sex for the first time. I wondered if it was some sort of nervous habit. All I knew is that whatever it was, it was pretty freaking adorable and was causing all of my remaining anger to melt away.

When I didn't immediately answer, Kinsley's face dropped and she went to turn around. "You probably don't. I'm sorry. Forget I mentioned it."

Before I could even process what had just happened, she was back in her room with the door shut. I hurried across the hall and opened her bedroom door without even knocking. "Of course I want to give Lenny a cookie and watch him take a bath. Why would I want to do anything else on a Friday night?"

The sweet smile on Kinsley's face in response to my words, made me want to grab that face and kiss it endlessly. I had to force myself to move that thought way to the back of my mind. We hadn't even technically made up yet. The last thing I should have been thinking about was kissing her. Kinsley reached into the little baggie she was holding and handed me the chinchilla cookie as if it were gold. "Now you can either tease him with it a little, or you can just hand it right to him through the bars. I, of course, tease him, but that's up to you."

I decided on the latter. If this chinchilla had to put up with Kinsley for the past 13 years, he deserved to get his treat without any struggle. I held the cookie up to the cage, and when he ran over to the spot where I was standing, slipped it through the bars. I squealed when he took the cookie in his tiny paws and began nibbling on it. "He is just so adorable," I beamed.

"Obviously. He *does* take after his mama." Kinsley followed her statement with a wink.

A few weeks ago this not-so-subtle brag would have driven me insane, but I was starting to find that it was one of the many personality traits of Kinsley's that I found charming. "Fishing for compliments?"

"Don't have to. I know you agree with me." Kinsley flashed me another smile that had me going weak in the knees. When I smiled back at her, ours eyes stayed locked on each other, and the air became thick with the best kind of tension. I'm not sure how long we stayed like this, but I wasn't willing to look away. There was more said in that moment than any words could have conveyed.

"Grace… I…" Kinsley finally broke eye contact to look toward the chinchilla cage. "I think this guy is ready for his bath."

I tried to hide my disappointment over the emotional shift in the room, by focusing on the chinchilla, who was now crawling into a tube filled with dust. Kinsley and I both laughed as he rolled around in the powdery mass. After a few minutes, Kinsley looked away from Lenny to look over at me. "Just so you know, this is my way of apologizing for being a jerk and for pulling away from you."

I feigned surprise. "Wait. Is Kinsley Scott actually trying to say sorry?"

She pushed her shoulder into mine. "Believe it or not, it does happen every once in awhile." Kinsley's whole demeanor then changed. "I really am sorry Grace. I'm honestly not so sure why you're still putting up with me, but I want you to know that I'm really happy that you are." The sincerity in her voice sent another whirlwind of emotions through me.

I laid my hand on top of hers and was happy when she didn't pull it away. "You're not a bad person Kinsley, no matter how much you want people to believe that."

Another quick moment passed between Kinsley and I before she started to chuckle. "It's the chinchilla, isn't it? He's the reason you keep coming back," she joked.

"Obviously. I'm just *dying* to know what this supersized penis looks like. It's actually been on my lesbian bucket list for years."

Kinsley cackled at my joke. "You're surprisingly funny when you want to be."

I tapped my nose against hers, forcing myself to back up instead of kissing her. "And you're surprisingly sweet."

"Speaking of being sweet, what do you say I order us Chinese, and then you can show me what this *Pretty Little Liars* is all about?" *Be. still. my. Heart.*

***

"So, you're telling me that you actually got Kinsley to watch, not just one, but *two* episodes of Pretty Little Liars?" Leah laughed as we sat at dinner with her and Liam the next night.

"Yep," I bragged. "And I totally think I could get her to watch the whole series." At least, I hoped that I could. I wanted to find any excuse that I could to snuggle close to Kinsley on the couch with her strong arm wrapped around me, just like I had last night.

Leah laughed even harder now. "Good luck with that. Kinsley has never committed to anything in her life."

I knew Leah was just messing around, but I couldn't help but feel defensive over Kinsley. I had no question that she had it in her to be the person that other people didn't see; the person that I was lucky enough to catch glimpses of. "That's actually not true," I pointed out. "She has been very dedicated to Lenny ever since she got him."

Leah stabbed a piece of steak onto her fork, then pointed it toward me. "That's a good point. She's had that rat forever."

"It's a chinchilla," Kinsley and I answered together.

Leah and Liam gave each other a look, then turned back toward us. "You two are freaking adorable when you're not trying to claw each other's eyes out." Leah's eyes lit up as if she had just had an epiphany. "By the way, Liam and I have to stay at our place tonight, so it's going to be a bit crowded. Sorry."

"We do?" Liam questioned.

"Yes. Remember? The apartment above yours flooded, and now there is water leaking from the ceiling in your bedroom?"

"Ouch. I mean duh. The flood. How could I forget the flood?"

I ignored Leah and Liam's strange interaction, because I was already running the logistics of the sleeping arrangement through my head. I knew where I desperately wanted to spend the night, but I wasn't going to suggest that. Nothing good ever came of Kinsley and I sleeping in close quarters. Ok, that wasn't true, but the fall out was always negative.

Kinsley gave me a reassuring smile and patted me on the knee. "No worries. I'll just sleep on the couch."
Really? She chose this time to be chivalrous?

"I can't make you do that," I argued. "I'll take the couch."

"Here's a crazy idea. Why don't you both just sleep in Kinsley's bed? It wouldn't be the first time, and I don't think any of us need to pretend it will be the last." Leah smirked across the table at us, clearly satisfied with herself for calling us out again.

Kinsley shrugged her shoulders. "I'm ok with it if you are."

Of course I was ok with it. I was more than ok with it. I tried to push aside the thoughts about what could happen while sharing her bed, because I knew there was something more important that needed to happen. This was going to be the perfect opportunity to finally address Kinsley's big confession.

Chapter 15: Kinsley

I groaned in response to Grace's question about my camping trip breakdown. Although, I had to admit, I was surprised it had taken her this long to bring it up. She certainly wasn't someone to just let things go, especially a meltdown of epic proportions like mine. I couldn't decide if she was a genius or just plain cruel for bringing it up once we were tucked into bed for the night.

"You don't have to tell me everything, but please just give me something, Kinsley."

I took a deep, calming breath. I wasn't used to allowing myself to be vulnerable, but I wanted to be that person for Grace. "You know how I told you that Lenny's full name is Lenny Lesden Scott?" Grace gave me a look that told me I better not be trying to avoid this topic by giving more useless facts about the chinchilla, but I shook my head. "I promise this is relevant. Lesden was the name of a chatroom I used to go in when I was a teenager. Yes, I do realize how weird and shady that sounds, but you have to realize that I was a lonely and scared baby gay trying to get by in a small town in the early 2000's."

"Hey, I'm not judging," Grace laughed. "At least you knew who you were."

"Barely," I scoffed. "I ended up meeting another teenage girl on there named Nikki Cramer. We started out as chat room buddies, which led to private messaging, and eventually, we exchanged numbers. She became one of my best friends. She was actually the person who encouraged me to buy Lenny, which is why I named him after the chatroom. It was my way of naming him after her without being overly obvious to my friends and family. Anyway, junior year we both admitted that we had feelings for each other. Nikki actually ended up coming out to her friends and family later that year, and she told me that we could be a couple if she felt like there was a chance that it could actually go somewhere. So, I told her that I would go to whatever college she wanted to go to so we could be together. I was madly in love at this point and would have done anything for her. Plus, I wanted to get as far away from my town as possible, so going to college a half hour from her Wisconsin hometown sounded like a good deal to me."

Grace listened intently as I spoke, hanging on to every word I said, which encouraged me to keep going. "I refused to tell anyone in my life why I had chosen that random college that I had never even gone to visit. I wouldn't even tell my grandma anything. I just packed up my things and never looked back, literally. It was actually a super dumb plan on my part, obviously. For all I knew, this girl was playing me or not who she said she was, but I refused to believe that could be the case. It turns out that it wasn't. She was exactly who she claimed to be. It truly felt like a real life fairytale. I was finally living my life as my authentic self, and I was actually accepted by her friends and family. They accepted me. They accepted our relationship. It was nothing like what I suspected my hometown would have been. I figured this was what the rest of my life was going to be."

"What happened?" Grace asked softly, running a finger over my cheek. I stared down at her other hand that was just barely resting on my hip. I wasn't sure how I was supposed to talk about this next part. How do you talk about the moment someone realizes that you're just not good enough for them? Grace brought her hand to my chin to force me to look up at her. When we were level with each other, she captured my lips with her own. It was one simple kiss, but conveyed so much, and gave me the strength I needed to go on.

"Nikki came from a very well off family. They owned this chain of shopping centers in their area. It was known that Nikki was going to go into the family business, and I realized once I grew closer to them, that they just kind of assumed that I would too. I was undecided, but they all figured I was eventually going to choose business. Truthfully, I figured that too until I took a creative writing class and fell in love. I never knew just how therapeutic it could be to get my thoughts down. When I told Nikki that I was going declare my major as English with a concentration on creative writing, she wasn't happy. I sat down with her family, and they convinced me I should at least make journalism my concentration instead, since apparently, that's *where the money is*. Even though I took their advice, things still changed after that. It was a slow change, that I think was slowed even more by how much it hurt me when my grandma died, but by the time we were at the end of our junior year, it was completely done. I didn't want to see it, so Nikki pulled the plug. She told me that she felt like our lives were going in different directions, but I know it was because she didn't believe my income or career choice was going to be good enough for her or her family."

Grace ran her hands up and down my arms, where goosebumps had started to form. "I'm so sorry Kinsley. I know how much it sucks when you feel like you're not good enough for someone, but just because one person thought that doesn't mean it's true. You're more than good enough."

After she spoke, I couldn't keep the tears from falling. "See, that's just the thing. I'm not good enough. Love ruined me. When I say that I turned around and never looked back, I mean I literally never looked back. I left for college and never went back home. I spent every holiday and break with

Nikki's family. I didn't want to go back and be surrounded by the people who didn't know the real me. I didn't want to be forced back into the closet. But in the process of trying not to hurt myself, I hurt every single other person in my life. My grandma used to call me every week and ask when I was coming home to visit. I would lie and tell her it would be soon, even though I had no intentions on actually going. Do you want to know when I finally saw her? It was at her viewing Grace. I didn't go home until she was already gone. And I didn't even go to the burial. After the funeral, I told my family that I would meet them there, but instead I got in my car and drove all the way back to Wisconsin. I couldn't stand the thought of facing them after what I had done to my grandma in the last two years of her life. I ran all the way back to the girl who ended up breaking my heart a year later. Love did that to me. It made me into a monster who lets people down. It made me into a sarcastic asshole who treats people like shit. It *ruined* me, Grace."

"Love didn't ruin you, Kinsley. It was infatuation and it was naivete, and it was even fear. But it wasn't love. Plus, you're not ruined. You might be a little bit broken, but you're far from ruined. I think you're amazing."

I laid in silence letting Grace's words sink in. Letting Grace sink in. For the first time, I let her take over me. I didn't try to push away the feelings that were building inside of me. My mind drifted away from Nikki and my past and became focused on one thing only. I knew exactly what I needed in that moment.

"Show me." It was a whispered request that could only be heard because of the utter silence surrounding us.

"Show you what?" Grace ran one lone finger along my cheek as she waited for my reply.

I sighed in response to her touch, then looked into those big green eyes. "Show me what sex is like when it's more than just sex."

Grace's eyes went wide, but she didn't move. "For sex to be more than just sex, there has to be feelings involved."

I put both of my hands on her cheeks and directed her lips to mine, slowly opening my mouth to hers. As I reluctantly pulled away just a few moments later, I hoped that kiss conveyed the feelings that I couldn't. "Please show me," I repeated once again.

This time, Grace nodded in understanding and brought our lips back together. The kiss was easy and unhurried, and Grace delicately ran her fingers along my sides as we continued to get lost in each other. There was nothing rushed about it, which was so unlike any sex I had experienced in the past. I honestly wondered if we would actually move past the kissing, until I felt Grace begin to tug on my shirt. She pulled back just a bit and kept her eyes plastered on mine as she lifted it over my head. I did the same with her shirt, and we repeated this process until every last bit of clothing was removed. It certainly wasn't the first time I had been naked in front of someone. It wasn't even the first time I had been naked in front of Grace, but as she grazed her eyes over my whole body, I had never felt more exposed.

She directed me to lay on my back, then began kissing along my jawline. Her lips moved at a painstakingly slow pace along my neck and across my chest. When I bucked below her, doing anything I could to feel more connected, she pulled back and shook her head while smiling slyly at me. As if that wasn't enough torture, she bit her bottom lip before bending down to take mine between her teeth.

As she began kissing me again, she explored my whole body with her hands, and I began to do the same. This would normally be the time that I would flip a girl over and go to town on her, but I was more than happy feeling out every single curve.

After a few more minutes, Grace pulled back again, straddling my waist as she stared right through me. For only a brief moment, she looked like she was starting to question what she was doing, but she swiftly returned to the confident girl that I certainly wasn't used to but was quickly growing very fond of.

She spread her legs and positioned herself between mine, then gently rocked against me. It wasn't the first time I had done this. At this point, I was pretty sure that I had tried every position out there, but this was different. It was so different. As we moved together, she took my chin in her hand and directed my eyes toward her.

"Look at me." It sounded so much more like a request than a demand leaving her lips. "You are so beautiful," she confessed breathlessly, before capturing my lips with hers.

The kiss was slow and sensual and in perfect rhythm with our bodies. I found myself getting closer to the edge as every single part of us became one, body and soul.

"It's time to let go, sweetheart," Grace spoke into my mouth, as she picked up her pace. I followed her lead and completely let go, allowing myself to feel everything. We reached climax together, both clinging on tight as the sensation rushed through us; the sounds of our shared orgasm muffled by our still connected mouths.

Grace kept her body resting on top of mine for the next few minutes, as we both lay in silence, the only sound in the room being the rapid beating of both of our hearts.

When she ultimately lifted off me, I rolled onto my side so I could look into her eyes. Her green eyes glowed in the dark room, and I found myself getting lost all over again. "Grace... I..."

"I know..." she reassured me. But I wasn't sure what it was that she knew exactly. I couldn't even figure out what I was feeling at the moment. Luckily, I didn't have to. Grace simply took me in her arms, and I buried my head in her chest as I drifted off to sleep.

Chapter 16: Grace

I half expected to wake up the next day and find that Kinsley had run away again. Actually, I more than half expected it. The night before had been *intense*, even for me. Kinsley's confessions were charged with emotion. And that sex. Wow. I had never in my entire life experienced something like that. That's because it wasn't sex. We made love. Can it be called that even if you aren't actively *in love* at the time? Because it definitely felt like that. Even in all of my years with Becky, it never once felt like that. The passion and fire was unmatched. But why hadn't it been like that with Becky? I was in love with her. Sure, I couldn't deny anymore that I had really strong feelings for Kinsley, but I certainly wasn't in love.

I felt her body, that was still wrapped around mine, stir next to me and held my breath as her eyes opened. This was the moment of truth. She slowly opened just one eye and stared over at me. "Are you seriously watching me sleep right now? Creeper." She then surprised me by pulling me in closer to her. I had no clue what was happening, but I also didn't want to ruin the moment by questioning it, so I simply leaned into her embrace.

Kinsley hummed in response to this interaction. "Morning sex?" she mumbled in her sleepy morning voice which I had just discovered was extremely sexy.

I sighed. Morning sex with Kinsley sounded great, but one of us had to be mature about this, and I figured it wasn't going to be her. "We should probably talk about last night."

As expected, Kinsley groaned in response. "It's way too early for talking."

I lifted an eyebrow and felt a smirk come onto my face. "And it's not too early for sex?"

"It's never too early for sex," Kinsley mumbled again. She then opened her second eye and blinked a few times to focus on me. She looked so good laying there naked beside me, and I knew my resolve wouldn't hold up for long.

"Let's say I *did* agree to have sex with you. Then would you talk to me?"

"Sex *and* breakfast. Then I'll talk."

"Fine. It's a deal," I agreed. The cute smirk on Kinsley's face over the belief that she had won, made my fake hesitance totally worthwhile. The reality of the situation was that I was actually the one who had won. I started my day out with a mind blowing orgasm, was served breakfast in bed that Kinsley voluntary got up to cook, and now she was going to have this conversation whether she liked it or not.

After taking her last bite, Kinsley sat down her fork and looked over at me with a serious expression on her face. "So, last night was…" I braced myself for her next words. *A mistake? A bad idea? A one time thing?* "Indescribable."

I let out a contented sigh in response to Kinsley's confession and pulled her in closer to me, laying my head on her chest. To my surprise, she naturally began running her hand through my hair, as if this was something that we did every morning. I found myself wishing that it was. "Care to elaborate?" I finally asked, when I realized that was all Kinsley was giving to me.

She groaned in response. "You're not going to make this easy on me, are you? So, as I said, last night was indescribable. I've never experienced sex like that before. It was by far the most passionate night of my life. There's no way that I can deny that I have feelings for you at this point. I find you sexy, funny, and mildly to severely infuriating depending on the day. You're also extremely smart, and you enjoy chinchillas, so what's not to like?"

When I smiled, Kinsley's face twisted into one of concern, and she shook her head. "What happened last night doesn't change how I feel about love and relationships. I'd really love to continue whatever this is, but I'm never going to be the person who changes her relationship status on social media and introduces you to people as my girlfriend, and that's not fair to you."

I considered Kinsley's words. While I did want to eventually settle down with someone, I wasn't looking for a relationship. I was still too messed up from Becky. "What if we just enjoyed each other?" I suggested. "Not try to make it into something that it's not, but also not deny what it is."

"Does enjoying each other include more sex?" Kinsley smirked.

I moved my body on top of hers so I was straddling her hips. "Oh yes. Lots and lots of sex," I purred, before bending down to kiss her. "Sex, Chinese food, pizza."

Kinsley raised both eyebrows and placed her hands on my hips. "I like all of those words."

I started to run a hand down the length of her body. "And, of course, there will be a lot of talking and opening up. Right, Kinsley?"

When she glared up at me, I stopped the path of my hand and smiled back. "Right, Kinsley?"

"If I agree, will you continue to move your hand to its original destination?"

"Possibly," I teased. "There's only one way to find out though." I gave Kinsley a flirtatious grin, really enjoying the fact that I had control for once.

"Fine," Kinsley conceded. "All of the talking. So much talking. Words galore."

Her words made me burst into laughter, but I began the path of my hand again. "Good girl."

Two orgasms later, Kinsley and I were snuggled on the couch watching TV. Leah's voice snapped us both away from the show. "I'm very happy to see that you two made up, or I guess maybe I should say that I was happy to hear that you made up." She followed her words with a fake gag.

I cringed at the thought of Leah hearing us last night and again this morning. We had never had the type of friendship where we were open with each other about our sex lives. Then again, back when we were really close, neither of us were having sex. "I'm sorry, Leah," I apologized. "We'll try to be more quiet next time."

Kinsley snickered next to me. "Don't apologize to her. Do you know how many times I've had to listen to Liam squeal like a little girl when they're having sex?"

Leah ignored Kinsley's comments and looked between the two of us instead. "So, does this mean you guys are officially dating now?"

I felt Kinsley's body stiffen below me. "Oh. No. We're not dating. We're just enjoying each other… exclusively." It made my heart beat faster to hear Kinsley add the word exclusively. I knew that I wouldn't be dating or hooking up with anyone else, but I honestly didn't know how she felt about that.

My swooning was interrupted by Leah's laughter. "Yeah, sweeties. That's called dating. But you two can call it whatever you want because you're super adorable together."

"Totally agree," Liam added as he joined us in the living room. He then put an arm around Leah. "Ready?"

I looked at my phone and saw that it was only 10. "Where are you two off to so early?"

"We're going back to Liam's for the day. We figured you two could use some time alone to *enjoy each other* today."

"I'm surprised you guys want to go back there with the leak," I commented, finally starting to catch on to why their interaction had seemed so strange when she brought it up at dinner last night.

"Leak?" *Busted.*

"Oh yeah. You know. The leak in the bedroom because of the apartment above flooding. I'm surprised they could get that fixed so fast." My voice dripped with sarcasm as Leah remembered her lie from the night before.

"Oh. The leak. Of course. Of course," she spoke quickly. "Big flood. Big leak. It's crazy how quickly the apartment complex worked to get it all fixed. Welp, we're going to go. You two have a good day." The two of them were out the door before I could say anything else.

I shook my head and looked over at Kinsley. "That little shithead," she laughed. To my surprise, she leaned in and gave me a kiss, as if it was the most natural move ever. "A shithead that I am very, very thankful for right now," she added. I snuggled even closer to Kinsley and breathed her in, feeling content to just spend time close to her.

***

This was how most of our time was spent over the next few weeks. Kinsley had to spend a few hours writing each day, and I used this time to consider job and housing options, and we also spent some time with Liam and Leah, but anytime it was just the two of us hanging out, we chose to stay in. Our conversations were light, never touching on the subject of Kinsley's past again. I was fine with that. I was just happy to not be constantly fighting with her. Sure, we still had dumb little arguments about what movie to watch or whether someone was cheating at a board game, but luckily since our sexual chemistry only seemed to get better with time, we had found creative ways to work out the tension.

One Wednesday afternoon, after Kinsley was done writing, she joined me on the couch and slinked one arm around my shoulders. "So, it turns out that today is the two month mark of you being in Philly. And before you get all swoony thinking I marked my calendar or something, the only reason I know is because of my Twitter. I tweeted about the Liberty Bell on your second day here. *That's* how I know."

I tapped my chin as if I was contemplating something. "Did you happen to scroll back through your tweets to see which day you posted that?"

To my surprise Kinsley's face actually turned the slightest bit red from my question. "Don't worry about how I figured it out, OK? That's not the point. The point is that I think we should celebrate. I'd like to take you out... of the apartment to celebrate. Just the two of us. On me."

I couldn't help but giggle at Kinsley's wording. The average person would just ask if you wanted to go on a date, realizing that a date didn't mean you had to spend forever together, but not Kinsley. "And where would you like to take me out?" I asked.

"I figured we could go to a nice restaurant. You know, maybe eat something other than Chinese and pizza."

"They make other food?" I joked.

"Believe it or not, they do. So I need you to meet me back out here around 5:00. Wear something nice."

At 5:00, I waited in the living room, wearing a knee-length, blue dress with white flowers on it and a brown belt around the waist. When Kinsley entered the room, I felt like I was going to have to pick my jaw up off the ground. She wore a simple, red dress that was about the same length as mine, but she looked amazing in it. Then again, I was starting to think that Kinsley Scott could look good in absolutely anything. Her hair had a bit of waviness to it, and she had half of it pulled back. When she smiled at me, her blue eyes shimmered even more than I had ever noticed before. She kept it no secret that she was sweeping those blue eyes over the entire length of my body, and it took all of my self-control to not suggest that we just stay in instead. When her eyes met mine again, she bit her lower lip and lifted a flirtatious eyebrow. "My, my, my. Don't you clean up well."

I nervously looked toward the ground and adjusted my glasses on my nose. Tonight may have marked two months of me being in Philly, but I was still the same no-chill nerd from that first night. I was starting to curse myself out for acting this way, when Kinsley walked over and put her hand under my chin, forcing me to look at her. She reached out and readjusted my glasses for me. "I need you to do me a favor and never ever start wearing contacts. Your eyes are stunning, but I just find it so damn charming when you play with your glasses like that. I know that you do it when you're nervous, and I love that I make you nervous."

Kinsley started to laugh, and I playfully pushed her away from me. "Now you're just being mean," I pouted.

Kinsley leaned in and took that lip between her teeth, slowly pulling and causing a million sensations to run through me. "Am I still mean?"

"Yes!" I gasped, trying to catch my breath. "That is very mean. You are forcing me out of the apartment tonight, but making me want to just stay in and rip this dress off of you."

Kinsley took a step back from me and wiggled her eyebrows. "Just so you know, I'm more than OK with that."

"Oh no, you don't. You promised me a lavish dinner. We can save the dress ripping for after."

"Only if you promise."

"Promise what?"

"That there will be actual dress ripping."

I rolled my eyes at Kinsley and forced her out of the apartment. As we walked through the streets of Philadelphia, Kinsley still refused to tell me where we were going. Finally, we arrived at a fancy looking restaurant I had never heard of before. "Have you ever been to a Brazilian Steakhouse?"

When I shook my head, Kinsley just laughed. "Oh, you're in for a treat. Get ready to have your mind blown." It turned out that Kinsley was pretty good at blowing my mind and this restaurant was no exception. A Brazilian steakhouse is like an all-you-can-eat meat buffet, and the best part is that you don't even have to get up from your table. As long as you turned the faux stoplight on the table to green, men dressed in very expensive looking suits would continuously stop by the table and offer all different types of chicken, steak, and sausage. Kinsley and I went to town, and our eyes lit up each time a new item was brought out. I don't think there was ever a time in history that two lesbians were so excited about a bunch of meat.

I found myself laughing out loud (and snorting) in response to my own internal joke. Kinsley tilted her head at me. "Mind sharing with me what is so funny that it turned you into Miss Piggy over there?"

When I felt myself turning red, Kinsley reached out her hand and squeezed mine. "A very, very adorable Miss Piggy of course. Have I mentioned that I also really enjoy how you snort uncontrollably? I find all of your geeky quirks extremely sexy."

This was shocking to me. Kinsley Scott was the definition of sexy. She was the type of girl who turned heads when walking into any room. She could have walked into a room full of gay guys, and all eyes would still be on her. It's just the type of presence she had. But, for whatever reason, she found awkward old me to be sexy.

"Shall we go?" Kinsley spoke, interrupting my thoughts. "I thought maybe we could take a walk through the city before heading back to the apartment."

I smiled across the table at her, still feeling awestruck that she wanted to do something as simple as that with me. "Sounds wonderful."

Once we were outside, an urge came over me to take Kinsley's hand, but I wasn't quite sure if public hand holding was kosher in whatever it was that we were currently doing. I cleared my throat a few times and looked over toward Kinsley. "So, I would really *enjoy* holding your hand right now. Is that... Umm... something that is OK to do?"

To my surprise, Kinsley reached out and immediately took my hand. "Of course it's OK. The best part of this arrangement is that there are no rules. If you want to hold my hand as we walk down the street, you can. If I want to dance with you in the middle of Philadelphia, I can." With those words, Kinsley used the hand she was holding to twirl me around in a circle. Once I was facing her, she pulled me in tight and swayed to the sounds of the city night. I rested my head on her chest, finding that I didn't care if anyone was watching us. It was just Kinsley and I in this moment. Everyone else faded away. Which is why I also didn't think anything of it when she desperately brought her mouth to mine and made out with me right in the middle of the sidewalk. When we finally pulled apart, her swollen lips had formed into a wide smile. "We need to get home. I believe I was promised some dress ripping."

By the time we had arrived back home, the food coma hit and within minutes, Kinsley was passed out on the bed snoring. There was clearly no dress ripping occurring. But, as I situated Kinsley's body so I could crawl into the bed beside her, I didn't care about that one bit. This right here was just as good.

Chapter 17: Kinsley

Just three days after our dinner, Grace informed me that she wanted to take me out as well. She wouldn't tell me what we were doing, but told me there was no need to dress up and that she actually encouraged sweats. My mounting curiosity piqued when Leah and Liam came to the apartment to give us the keys to Liam's truck. "Is it totally ready for us?" Grace prodded seriously.

"Just as you ordered, my queen," Liam joked, adding in a fake bow for good measure.

Grace let out a cute squeal and pulled him into a tight hug. "Thank you so much for doing that."

Leah rolled her eyes at the interaction. "Don't let him fool you. It was all me. I'm all about making sure you guys *enjoy each other*," she mocked.

"Well, thank you both," Grace grinned. "We'll definitely enjoy it. At least I hope so."

She looked to me for confirmation, and I nodded my head even though I had no clue what was going on. The truth was that it didn't really matter what we were doing. I knew it would be fun because I always had fun when Grace was involved. Normally, I would have found this fact concerning, but I was honestly enjoying myself too much to care.

We said our goodbyes to Leah and Liam, then headed to our unknown destination in Liam's truck. A little over an hour later, I saw a sign that read *Old Tyme Drive-In.* "No way," I screamed. "I haven't been to the drive-in movies in forever. We actually had one of these about a half hour from my house, and I loved it when I was younger."

Grace grabbed my hand and squeezed, causing me to momentarily lose my breath. "I was hoping that was the case. I kind of figured it might be since you're a small town girl. This is actually the one I used to come to as a kid. We're about 25 minutes from my hometown right now."

Grace laughed as I raised an eyebrow at her. "I know what you're thinking, and don't worry, I didn't bring you out here to meet the folks. You're totally safe." Of course she had read my mind. Grace seemed to be able to do that. Although, being so close to Grace's hometown did give me the strange urge to go explore it. I wanted to see where she went to school and where she liked to hang out. I was interested to know exactly what shaped her into the girl she was today, which is exactly why it was probably good we weren't doing that. Those were a lot of lines that I shouldn't be crossing.

Grace backed the truck into a parking spot so the tailgate was facing the screen. Once she unlatched it, I realized that there had been an air mattress set up with blankets and pillows to lay on while we watched the movies. If I was the type of girl to swoon, I would have been swooning in that moment.

Once we were all situated under the blankets, my mind flashed back to the last time I was at the drive-in. Thinking of these memories filled me with equal amounts of sadness and happiness. "You know, the last time I was at the drive-in was actually with my grandma," I divulged.

Grace looked over at me with apologetic eyes. "Oh Kinsley, I'm sorry. I didn't know…"

I shook my head. "No. No. This is a good thing. It brings back all happy memories of my grandma. We used to go to the drive-ins together a lot. I think the last time we came was when I was in 8th grade. I lost interest when people from my class used to come just so they could hook up. I didn't really want to be sitting in a car with my grandma when my classmates were in the car next to us giving hand jobs under a blanket."

When Grace laughed softly at my words, I felt myself becoming overwhelmed with emotions. She was beautiful when she laughed, and right now, she was laughing with me over how pathetic I was as a teenager. I never shared these stories with anyone, and the way she was responding to them was exactly how I hoped someone would. I forced these thoughts from my head. There was no reason to be getting all sentimental. "Just so you know, I'm not that girl anymore. I'm totally ok with you getting handsy under this blanket," I joked, feeling more like myself again.

"What kind of girl do you think I am? We are at a family establishment surrounded by children." Grace's teasing tone told me that she wasn't actually offended by my words.

"I'm honestly not sure what type of girl you are, Just Grace. One day you're telling me that you were practically saving yourself for marriage, and then suddenly, it's last night and you're begging me to…"

Grace slapped a hand against my mouth before I could continue. "Some things that happen in the heat of the moment, should stay there and never be brought up again." Even though it was dark, I could tell that her face was just as red as her hair. I ran my tongue along the hand that was still over my mouth.

Grace tore it away and wiped it off on her sweatpants. "Ew. Who said you could lick me?"

Oh, this girl made it way too easy to mess with her. "Technically, you did this morning," I smirked.

The shades of red continued to deepen as she shoved my shoulder. "What did I just say?" she whisper-scolded. She then turned away from me, but instead of looking toward the movie that had just started, she laid on her back and looked up at the sky. "The stars look beautiful tonight."

I joined her, laying on my back as well and reaching out to take her hand. "This is one thing I miss about small town life. All of the lights of the city really drown out the stars."

"Well, aren't you quite the romantic?"

"Ew, no. Just because I can appreciate the stars, doesn't mean I'm a romantic. I'm a romance writer. It's my job to appreciate this stuff."

"Kinsley," Grace whispered, her voice now serious. "I don't want to push anything, and I want you to know that this doesn't change a thing about what we are or what we're doing, but nights like tonight and Wednesday just seem too special to not acknowledge them for what they truly are - a date."

Grace must have noticed the way my body tensed up in response to that word, because she grasped my hand a little tighter. "Calling this a date doesn't mean that we need to start planning our wedding or even planning for next week. It just acknowledges the fact that this moment right here is special."

Between the stars, my memories, and her words, I thought I might actually start to cry. The sensation was both scary and freeing at the same time. I was falling hard and fast for this girl, but like she said, I wasn't planning a wedding or even a future for that matter. I was completely capable of enjoying this feeling while it lasted and leaving it at that. I realized that as I was lost in my thoughts, Grace was watching me intently, waiting for an answer. "I think it's perfectly acceptable to call this a date." I brought our linked hands up to my lips and kissed her knuckles. Except it didn't actually feel acceptable to call it a date. Time with Grace shouldn't be reduced to a term also used by horny teenagers at a school dance. *Shit, I was losing it.*

Grace squeezed my hand, interrupting my internal dialogue once again. "What is going on inside that head of yours?" she asked. "I know you're not watching the movie because your eyes are closed."

"Here's the thing. I could tell you now or show you later."

"Fine," Grace conceded, leaving us in silence again.

Silence with Grace was oddly comfortable, but I also found myself longing to share more with her. "My grandma's birthday is next Friday," I finally spoke into the silence. "I spent every single birthday with her up until college. I still feel guilty about missing those last two."

Grace pulled me closer and buried her face into my neck, saying more with that action than any words could have said. I leaned in close and we stayed like this for a few minutes, until Grace suddenly sat up, staring down at me. "So I have an idea. Please don't get freaked out. You can absolutely say no. But what if you and I visited your grandma's grave on her birthday? I know you probably think I'm crazy, but I just thought maybe it would be good for you to spend that time with her. And I'd like to be there to support you. That is, if you want me there."

My mind started to spin from just thinking about her idea. What made her think that she even had the right to suggest that? She was correct about one thing though. I absolutely did think she was crazy for suggesting it. Asking me to do something that was clearly going to be hard for me was a sure fire way to get me to pull away. But it was also the sweetest damn thing that anyone had ever volunteered to do for me, so the following Friday afternoon I found myself driving Grace and I back to my hometown.

"Just so you know, my town is really small. I do love my family, but they're a bunch of rednecks," I warned Grace. Somehow, our day trip to my grandma's grave had turned into a weekend visit with my family. That was my fault for mentioning it to my mom when she called me the other day to see if I was doing OK. I should have known that she wouldn't have let me come without her seeing me, since my presence in this area wasn't a normal occurrence.

"Kinsley, calm down," Grace laughed. "Have you forgotten that I'm also from a small town? My parents are obsessed with me and are 100% supportive of me being gay, and they *still* voted for Trump. I get it."

"So, how did you and Leah become friends?" I asked, wanting to change the subject so I didn't have to think about everything that was coming.

A reminiscent smile appeared on Grace's face. "I feel like we've been friends forever. We grew up on the same street, just a few houses down from each other. From the time we were five or six, we did everything together."

My mind shifted to Leah talking about how they were childhood best friends, and I wondered when things had changed between them. "So, how did you guys end up drifting apart? I remember Leah saying that you guys hadn't seen each other much in the past few years."

"We stayed pretty close throughout the time we lived in our hometown. In high school, we each had a different core group of friends. Leah was a cheerleader and liked to party, while I was more into sports and academics at that point. We were still close though. You know how it is in a small town. But once we went away to college, we just kind of drifted. Nothing specific happened. Life just got in the way. Leah is the type of friend that I could see every day or once every two years and there would be no difference. We always just pick up right where we left off."

"I never had a friend like that," I admitted. I never gave anyone enough of a chance to form a bond like that. Just like romantic relationships, I was afraid if I got too close to a friend that it would hurt me too much to lose them. I hated the thought of losing someone because I didn't measure up to someone's expectations. Leah was by far the closest I had gotten to someone since my grandma and Nikki, but I even had a lot of walls up with her.

"How about you and Leah? How did you guys become friends?" Grace returned the question.

I started to laugh, thinking back on that time a few years ago. "I actually hit on her in a bar, believe it or not."

Grace lifted an eyebrow at me. "Elaborate, please."

"So, after about a year of living at home, I connected with this girl who helped me get my book into some libraries and other LGBT spots throughout the country. Her name is Rory. She's ridiculously smart and developed this whole app to connect small businesses with big businesses and so forth. It wasn't in her normal scope to do what she did for me, but she is also gay, so it was important to her. Plus, she was still getting things off the ground at that point. Anyway, we sort of became friends because we were both lady killers, so I came down to visit her a few years ago, and we went to the same club I took you to. Of course, Leah was there, which isn't shocking. She *would* be that basic straight girl who chose to hang out at a gay bar. When I tried hitting on her, she told me she was straight then jokingly said 'I'm not looking for a girlfriend, but I am looking for a roommate. Pretty close, right?' The rest was history after that. A few months later, I left my hometown to move in with this girl that I barely knew and almost seven years later, here we are."

Grace let out a low whistle at the realization of how long Leah and I had been roommates. "You guys are practically in a common law marriage at this point. What happened to the other girl? Rory? You said you guys were friends, but I haven't seen or heard anything about her in the two months I've been here."

I rolled my eyes thinking about Rory and what a sucker she was. "She lives in LA now. She fell madly in love and moved across the country for a girl. Apparently, it worked out for her though. She recently got engaged."

"Aw that's so sweet," Grace gushed. "What an adorable love story." I only grunted in response. Grace and I had grown so close that sometimes I forgot just how different we were. I should have known that she would somehow find that pathetic story sweet.

I became quiet as we got closer to the cemetery, completely lost in my own thoughts. There were a lot of different directions this could take, and I was worried about how I was going to respond to it. After parking, I led the way to her grave. I knew where it was since she was buried beside my grandpa, and I had visited his grave with her many times while growing up. I laid down the flowers we had bought on our drive and stared at the gravestone that I had avoided for the past ten years. My eyes wouldn't move from the name in front of me. I was laser focused, following the curves of every letter. My eyes moved back and forth across the letters about a thousand times until I wasn't able to focus on them anymore. The focus was replaced by a blur, which I soon realized was from the tears that had started to fall from my eyes.

Soon, I felt a hand latch onto mine and looked over to Grace standing next to me. "I… Umm... I'm not quite sure what I'm supposed to do."

"Talk to her."

"You want me to talk to a stone with words carved into it?"

Grace smiled sweetly and gave my hand an extra squeeze. "No, I want you to talk to your grandma. Say the things that you left unsaid."

I took a deep breath and looked back at the grave. "Sup, Grams. I'm not really sure what I'm supposed to say. My lady friend here tells me that I should talk to you though. First of all, in case you didn't realize this, I'm gay. But I guess if you're truly watching over me all the time, then you know that. If that is the case, I'm sorry by the way. You've probably seen a lot of shit you'd rather not see. What can I say? I got needs." I laughed awkwardly, before taking another deep breath, hoping I could make it through the next part without completely breaking down. "What I really wanted to say is that I'm sorry that I let you down. You were my best friend, and I should have been there for you at the end. I was running away from a life that scared me, but I shouldn't have run away from you. You were always there for me, and I hope you know how much I appreciated that. I still think about you everyday. I love you. Happy birthday."

Once the words were out, I leaned down to run a hand over the grave. Emotions overtook me, and I collapsed onto the ground, placing my head against the stone. Grace sat beside me and put an arm around my shoulder. "Shh, it's OK," she soothed, as I continued to repeat the words *I'm sorry* over and over again. She placed a kiss on my temple and began to run her hand up and down my back. I allowed myself to melt into her, as we sat in silence. I wasn't sure if we sat like this for a few minutes or a few hours, but it didn't matter. All that mattered was the moment that we were sharing.

Our silence was broken when I heard Grace whisper "L.S.." under her breath. It was barely audible and I wasn't sure she even meant to say it out loud, but I looked over at her for an explanation. "Sorry. I just had a realization. Your grandma's initials were LS. You dedicated your first book to her."

I wasn't sure whether to be flattered or creeped out that Grace remembered this, but I couldn't say that I was exactly surprised. For the first time since arriving, I let out a slight laugh. "Creep," I muttered playfully.

Luckily, Grace chuckled in response. "Whatever. I read that book more times than I'd like to admit. I probably have every word memorized." Grace hesitated then added, "I'm sure she is by the way."

"Is what?"

"Proud of you." Her reminder made the words from my dedication pop into my mind. *For L.S. - I love you and hope I'm making you proud.*

"I'm not so sure of that," I admitted, turning around so I was now looking out over the hillside that my grandma's grave sat on. "My grandma was one of a kind. She was so unapologetically herself. She didn't care what anyone else thought. I don't think I could ever measure up to that."

Grace turned so she was looking out over the hill with me now. "I don't know, Kinsley. If what you're saying is true, then it sounds like you are a lot like her."

"Hardly," I scoffed. "You were right in your assessment that first night we hung out. I'm a fraud. Laurel Lake and Kinsley Scott are two very different people and I play the part of both of them."

"And which one of them is the real you?"

I sincerely considered her question. Not long ago, I would have said that it was obviously Kinsley, but now I wasn't so sure. "Honestly? I'm not sure if either is. I understand the feelings I'm writing about in my books because I've felt them before, but that still doesn't mean that I actually believe them. Even if I somehow fell madly in love, I would still find the idea of *happily ever after* to be complete bullshit. Life is messy. It will always be messy, whether you find someone to spend it with or not. Things don't magically fall together and stay that way just because you meet *the one*, or say '*I love you*' for the first time, or even get married. Life will still find ways to test you or completely screw you over. So, I guess you could say that I fall somewhere in the middle. The rainbows, butterflies, and words of wisdom that Laurel Lake spews are shit. But Kinsley Scott isn't nearly as hard and callous as she pretends to be."

Grace stared into my eyes as if she was looking straight into my soul. "Have you ever considered that maybe you should stop playing those parts and just be *you?*"

I looked toward the setting sun, trying to will myself not to start crying again. "I'm not so sure I can do that. I feel like I've only been completely authentic with two people my entire life."

Grace continued to keep her eyes glued to me. It was so intense that I almost felt the need to squirm away, like her intensity could somehow burn me. "Your grandma and Nikki?" she finally asked. Although, it almost sounded more like a statement than a question.

I shook my head in response. "No. My grandma and..." I took another deep breath, unsure if I really wanted to admit this part. "And you."

For the first time since arriving, it looked like Grace might be the one to start to cry. Instead, her eyes moved from mine down to my lips and then her own lips followed that path as well, crashing into mine as softly as they could while still showing desperation. I ran my tongue along her lower lip, aching to feel more connected to her. As she opened her mouth to mine, I couldn't help the tiny moan that escaped me. This kiss, right here in the middle of a damn cemetery, charged with all of the emotion from the day, put every other kiss of my entire life to shame. I never wanted it to end, but eventually, Grace pulled back.

She started to giggle as we both took in our surroundings. I put my head in my hands, then turned to look at my grandma's grave once again. "By the way Grams, we do that… a lot. This girl is… well, she's something. You'd like her."

This time, a few tears did fall from Grace's eyes. She looked away from me, staring out at the setting sun. "This is one of the most beautiful sunsets I've ever seen." She looked back over at me, with a gleeful smile now on her face. "Could we take a picture?"

"Of the sunset or of us?"

"Both silly."

"Absolutely not," I groaned. "I've been crying all afternoon. I probably look like ass right now."

"For the record, you look beautiful. You always do. You have sunglasses though, right? Just put those on. Then there won't be any evidence of the crying."

"Instead I'll just look like a douche who wears sunglasses when it's dark out," I laughed.

A serious look took over Grace's face. "It's not dark yet. Technically, the sun is just as dangerous, or likely even more dangerous, to the eyes as it's rising and setting." She reached into her purse and pulled out a glasses case, replacing her current glasses with a pair of sunglasses. "Plus, you won't be alone."

I shook my head, my laugh becoming more hearty. "You are such a nerd. You did that on purpose, didn't you? You knew I wouldn't be able to say no to you when you're being all geeky and sexy?"

Grace simply laughed in return and pulled out her phone. I put on my sunglasses, and we turned so the sunset was behind us. I snaked my arm around her waist, and she put her free arm over my shoulder, leaning the weight of her body against me. I allowed myself to lean into her as well and smiled a genuine smile as she snapped the picture. She held the phone away from me while she studied her work. "This is great! Do you mind if I post it?"

"Just as long as you don't put some lame lovey dovey caption or inspirational quote, I'm fine with it."

Grace typed a few words, then showed me her phone. "How is that?"

I looked at the caption and started to laugh once again. I was starting to realize that I tended to do that a lot around Grace. "*Sunsets and shades*? Really? That's what you came up with?"

Grace shrugged her shoulders. "It's not my fault that you put a limit on my creativity. Plus, I happen to think it describes the moment perfectly." She continued to look down at the picture before smiling over at me. "The sunset truly does look very beautiful here, doesn't it?"

I nodded my head, even though that wasn't what had caught my eye. The sunset was far from the most beautiful part of that picture.

Chapter 18: Grace

"This girl is something." Those were the words that kept running through my head as Kinsley drove us to her childhood home. I knew it was just a dumb phrase, but coming from Kinsley, I also knew that it meant more. I wanted to know exactly what it meant, but asking her would have crossed a line that we agreed not to cross.

"So, I think I need to tell you a little bit more about my relationship with my family before we get there," Kinsley spoke nervously, interrupting my thoughts. "When I told you that I shut out the world once I realized I was gay, I meant that. It's especially true for my family. I shut them out while I was in high school, and as I told you, the only time I came home during college was that one time for my grandma's funeral. I didn't even come home when my nephew was born or two years later, when my niece was born. Even after Nikki dumped me, I didn't come home. I closed myself off from everybody, including my college friends since they had all been Nikki's friends first and foremost, and pretty much locked myself away for the last year and a half. One positive is that I wrote my first book at that time, but I didn't end up coming home again until after I graduated."

"Wait a second." I felt bad interrupting Kinsley's story, but all of this just sounded so familiar. That's when it hit me. "Your first book… that was about you and Nikki."

"My first book was fiction," Kinsley answered sharply. "All of them are."

"But it was based off of you and Nikki. Just admit it Kinsley. I don't know how I didn't realize it before now. The characters were named Kenzie and Nicole. The story is about the two of them being in a long distance relationship until Kenzie decides to move to Nicole. Then Nicole gets cold feet at one point and dumps her. But…"

"But it has a happy ending so it clearly wasn't about us," Kinsley interrupted, a bite to her voice now.

I knew I shouldn't push it, but I had learned that sometimes that's exactly what Kinsley needed. "It has the happy ending that *you* wanted. After being dumped, Kenzie moved back home, but Nicole came after her. She flew across the country and showed up at her door to win her back. That's how you wanted your story to end. You ran away, but you were hoping that Nicole would chase after you, weren't you?"

Kinsley's face turned red and I noticed that she had started to grip the steering wheel harder. "It doesn't matter what I was hoping for because it didn't happen. So just drop it, OK?! We have more important things to discuss right now."

I shrunk down into my seat, realizing I had pushed that too far. I had a tendency of doing that. I had pushed Becky right into the arms of another woman. I felt blush spread onto my cheeks. "Sorry. Please go on."

Kinsley gritted her teeth. "So, as I was saying before you rudely interrupted me, I spent four years acting like I didn't give a damn about these people. Sure, I talked to my parents when they called, and they even came out to visit once during my freshman year and one more time my sophomore year. Aside from from that, they got nothing from me. You know I'm not proud of that, but I haven't gotten much better since. I honestly still don't know how they feel about me being gay, so I have continued to keep them at arm's length."

I studied Kinsley, trying to decipher how she felt about this. Aside from her grandma, her attitude toward her family always seemed so indifferent, but I didn't think that was truly the case. I was starting to learn that Kinsley ran away when she cared too much, not the other way around. "How did your family react when you came out?" I hoped my question wouldn't cause Kinsley to shut down again.

"I wouldn't say I came out to my family. It was more like I tore that closet door off completely and didn't look back to check on the destruction I caused." Kinsley actually chuckled a bit when she said this. "I came home from school after graduation and I believe my exact words were, 'I'm gay and I don't want to hear what you have to say about it because I really don't care.' That was it. No one has said a word about it since. It's just the big rainbow elephant in the room anytime we're all together."

"Seems a little harsh, don't you think? No offense, Kinsley, but I feel like you didn't give them a chance."

Kinsley smiled at me in a way that I couldn't read. I honestly didn't know if she found my words amusing or if she was happy about the fact that she was about to go off on me. "You know… you have this really annoying habit of calling me out on my shit, and I can't decide if I love it or hate it. I agree though; it was harsh. And like I've said before, I really do adore my family. They've just never done anything to make me believe that they would be accepting of this part of my life, so it's easier to remain naive to how they really feel."

"I get it," I sighed. "My parents had a really hard time when I came out. They didn't want to accept it right away. It was definitely hard on all of us. They eventually came around though, and since then they have been 100% supportive. Maybe you should give your family a chance. I mean, they haven't turned their backs on you or disowned you. That has to count for something."

Kinsley shrugged her shoulders. "I guess so." She then turned onto the street marked *Hidden Lake Road,* and soon, we were pulling into her driveway. I looked at the modest two-story house in front of us. It was simple but cute. "Welp. Home sweet home," she muttered, before jumping out of the car and heading toward the door.

As soon as she opened the door, I could smell the scent of a home cooked meal wafting from the kitchen. My mouth immediately began to water. That was definitely one thing I missed since coming to Philly. I couldn't remember the last time I had a home cooked meal. Becky had always cooked, and then my mom took over that duty once I moved back home. Kinsley directed me to follow her and the smell continued to get stronger until we were in the kitchen. There was a woman standing by the stove, mixing something that appeared to be mashed potatoes. She was wearing an apron, and from behind, looked like a shorter, slightly more plump version of Kinsley. A blonde girl, who seemed to be a just few years older than us, entered the room carrying a stack of plates, napkins, and silverware. "Hey, Kinsley! When did you guys get here?" the blonde asked.

Upon hearing this, the older woman, who I assumed to be Kinsley's mom, whirled around. "Kinsley! My baby girl! I can't believe you're actually here," she squealed. She quickly made her way over to us and wrapped Kinsley in a big hug. When she pulled back, she continued holding onto her arms and studied her for a minute. "Are you eating enough? You're way too skinny."

Kinsley rolled her eyes at this. "Yes, mom. I eat all the time."

"You haven't become one of those people who doesn't eat meat, have you?" her mom asked skeptically.

"A vegetarian? No. You ask me this every time you see me, and the answer is always the same."

Her mom waved a hand at her. "Hey, you can't blame me for asking. You're a city girl now. I don't know how that will change you. Cities are filled with hippies and organic grocery stores and *Democrats*." She said the last word as though it was a curse word, rather than a political party. She then turned to look at me for the first time. "Oh goodness. Where have my manners gone?! I'm Mrs. Scott. You must be Grace."

I reached my hand out to her. "Yes. I'm Grace Harper. It's very nice to meet you Mrs. Scott."

Mrs. Scott grabbed my hand with both of hers and shook it enthusiastically, then continued to hold it as she leaned in to place a kiss on my cheek. Her lips then moved toward my ear and she loudly whispered, "I hear you're the one who convinced my daughter to actually come home this weekend. Thank you for that. She never wants to see her old mom."

Kinsley rolled her eyes again. "Mom, you know I can hear you, right?"

I playfully elbowed her in the side. "Hey! Be nice to your mother." Kinsley stuck her tongue out at me, and for a moment, I got caught up looking into her eyes, almost forgetting where we were. When I looked back at her mom, I realized her face had grown more serious, and she was looking between Kinsley and I, almost as if she was calculating something. I worried that she had seen our little moment and caught on to the fact that there was something going on between us, and the look on her face had me worried that maybe Kinsley's suspicions were right.

Luckily, the smile quickly returned to her face, and she winked over at me. "I can already tell that I'm going to like you," she chuckled.

By this time, the blonde had finished setting the table and made her way over to us. She smiled at me sweetly and reached out a hand. "I'm Kinsley's sister-in-law, Megan. It's nice to meet you, Grace." She then turned toward Kinsley. "It's great to see you Kinsley."

"Right back atcha," Kinsley replied. "I didn't realize you guys were going to be here tonight. Where is everyone else?"

"Of course they would be here!" Mrs. Scott answered excitedly. "It's not very often that we get to do family dinner together!"

Kinsley and Megan exchanged a look in response to Mrs. Scott's enthusiasm. "Your dad and brother are out back grilling steak, and I believe my children are glued to their iPads somewhere."

Kinsley used her head to motion toward the backyard. "Come with me. I'll introduce you to the rest of the fam." To my surprise, she instinctively reached out and grabbed my hand, dropping it almost immediately when she realized what she had done. Kinsley didn't blush very often, but her face was beet red as we walked out of the kitchen. It was absolutely adorable and made me wish that she was still holding my hand.

We made our way out her back door onto a large patio where two men in coveralls, that read *Scott Auto Body* in big bold letters, were perched over the grill. When they heard the door close, both men turned toward the sound. The older man's face lit up when he saw us. "Look who decided to come home!" he beamed. "Come give your old man a hug."

As Kinsley hugged her dad, the guy who I had to assume was her brother came over and gave her a noogie. "How's it going, kiddo?"

Kinsley pulled away from both of them, fixing her hair as soon as she was free. "I'm doing good. This is my uh… friend… Grace, by the way."

Grace's dad stuck his hand out to me. "Grace. Great to meet you. I'm Mr. Scott."

"And I'm Kevin," her brother added with a wave. "Sorry about the appearance. We were working late tonight. Didn't get the chance to go home and shower before the ladies demanded that we put on the steak. Speaking of which - it's done. Shall we head inside?"

When we got back to the kitchen, a little boy who looked to be around 10 or 11 and a girl who I assumed must have been about two years younger than him, given what Kinsley had told me in the car, were sitting at the table, completely entranced by the iPads in front of them. Kevin playfully tousled the little boy's blonde hair. "Could you put that damn thing away and give your aunt a hug please?" He then pointed over at the little girl. "Same goes for you, princess."

Both children jumped down from their seats and each hugged Kinsley from opposite sides. When they were done, she put her arms around them and looked over at me. "Tommy and Jane - this is my friend Grace." They each said a shy hello, while they leaned further into Kinsley. Watching her with them made me miss my own niece. Turns out, that was another thing that I missed about home.

Soon, we were all seated around the kitchen table, and as soon as Mr. Scott said a short prayer, everyone started to eat. My phone started to ring just a few minutes later, and I pulled it out to find it was my mom calling. "I'm really sorry," I apologized. I need to take this. If I don't answer, she'll get worried."

Mrs. Scott reached her hand out toward me. "Why don't you let me take it, dear?"

I probably would have found the gesture very strange if it wasn't something that I'm sure my own mother would have done. "No mom…" Kinsley began to protest, but I stopped her.

"It's ok. It gives me a chance to keep eating these delicious mashed potatoes." Kinsley rolled her eyes, and I honestly wasn't sure if she was rolling them because of my brown nosing or because her mom was currently leaving the room with my phone up to her ear, already chatting away.

About five minutes later, she returned to the room, phone still to her ear, laughing over something being said on the other end. "Yes, I'll tell her you said hello. Give Jim my best." I tried to stifle a laugh at the interaction. Jim was my dad's name. How had Kinsley's mom somehow gotten on a first name basis with my dad after just five minutes on the phone with my mom?

Mrs. Scott sat back down at the table and handed my phone over to me. "Your mother says hi and she misses you." I smirked at Kinsley who simply shrugged her shoulders in response.

"So, Grace, where are you from?" Mr. Scott inquired.

I looked down at my plate for a moment, nervous about being the center of attention. When I looked back up, I readjusted my glasses, and when Kinsley saw this, she placed a gentle hand on my knee and smiled over at me, immediately making me feel better. "She's from a small town in Maryland, but has been staying with Kinsley and Leah this summer," Mrs. Scott answered before I could.

"Seriously, mom?" Kinsley asked, bemused.

"Calm down dear. Carol told me." Carol. My mother. Somehow in the five minutes these ladies had talked, Mrs. Scott learned both of my parents' names and my residential history.

"Small town girl, huh?" Mr. Scott asked, ignoring the interaction between his wife and daughter. "I think you'll really enjoy what we are doing tomorrow night!"

"Do I even want to know what that is?" Kinsley groaned.

"Your brother started racing again, so we're going to the track. Grace, have you ever been to any sort of races before?"

"My dad and I have gone to Dover for a few NASCAR races." Kinsley lifted an eyebrow in response to my answer, and I wasn't sure if she was impressed or disgusted by my redneck response.

Mr. Scott just laughed. "This ain't NASCAR. You're in for a real treat."

***

He wasn't kidding. The small dirt-covered track that we arrived at the next night certainly wasn't anything like the speedway my dad and I had gone to growing up. Mr. Scott drove a big trailer right into the center of the track where a bunch of other trailers and race cars were parked. Kinsley's sister in law had stayed home with the kids, so it was just me and the immediate Scott family. Once we were out of the car, Mr. Scott put his arm around Kinsley and took in his surroundings. "This brings back a lot of memories, doesn't it? I can't remember the last time you were here with me."

"I spent a lot of time here growing up," Kinsley explained, leaving it at that. I wanted her to tell me more. I wanted to know all of the details of her childhood. I wanted every single memory - good and bad. But I also knew that was too much to ask for from Kinsley. I could only have Kinsley in pieces, and I had to be happy with that.

"So, where do we watch from?" I asked, looking around what I figured must be considered the pit area, and realized I couldn't see much of anything over all of the cars and trailers.

Kinsley slipped a hand over my shoulder and pointed toward a ladder attached to the side of the trailer. "That's the fun part. We get to go up there. I hope you're not afraid of heights." She laughed as she let her arm drop and sprinted toward the trailer. I wasn't able to move because I was so entranced watching her. I loved the childlike, carefree side of Kinsley. The way her eyes lit up when she was excited over something was absolutely breathtaking. "Are you coming?" she yelled over to me from halfway up the ladder.

Once I got past the nerves of scaling up the side of a trailer, I loved being up there. I was much more of a small town girl than I had ever admitted to Kinsley and felt in my element here. Aside from my time in Philly this summer, I had only ever lived in small towns, even during college. Kinsley smiled over at me. "So, what do you think?"

"I love it!" I answered a bit too enthusiastically, earning a loud cackle from Kinsley.

She walked over to me and began wiping her hands over my jeans. "You already have dirt all over you though. It's only going to get worse once the races start. I hope you can handle it."

I scoffed at her words. "Trust me, I can handle a little dirt. I think you've forgotten that you've been a city girl for years. I'm still technically a country girl. Living in Philly for two months ain't gonna change that."

Kinsley laughed at my words and moved her hands up to rest on my hips. Her eyes scanned the length of my body, making me wish for the first time of the night that we were anywhere but here right now. I had gotten so used to kissing Kinsley whenever I wanted that holding back was killing me right now. From the way Kinsley was staring into my eyes, I could tell she had the same thought. "I almost forgot," she announced, jumping back to grab something out of the backpack she had brought along. I immediately found myself missing the feeling of having her close, but I didn't have to miss it for long. Kinsley walked back to me, carrying some sort of safety glasses. She slipped them over the glasses already on my face and gave me a satisfied grin. "Can't have your glasses getting dirty on you." I felt like she was looking into my soul as she playfully adjusted the glasses. "My little nerdy redneck. Just when I thought you couldn't get any cuter." She let her hands drop from the glasses and burned a path down my arms, before resting back on my hips. Her eyes fluttered to my lips, and I felt her body moving even closer to mine. Kinsley's hands dropped, and her body stiffened when we heard people climbing up the side of the trailer. By the time her family was up there with us, there was a large gap between us. I wasn't used to this unsure, nervous side of Kinsley. It was so different than the confident girl I usually saw. I didn't like this version any less though. If anything, I found this side of her endearing. Although, I hated the fact that it was caused by her lack of confidence in her family's acceptance.

"Who wants a beer?" Kinsley's voiced boomed, as she became herself again. She popped the beer can open and held it out to me.

I shook my head and tried not to make a face. "No thanks. I don't drink beer."

"Of course you don't." Kinsley grinned, before taking a big sip of it herself.

I felt a hand on my arm and looked over to see Mrs. Scott standing next to me. "Don't worry dear. I have us covered." She reached into her big purse and pulled out a bottle of wine and two solo cups, pouring some for each of us.

Kinsley tapped her can against my cup. "Cheers to Pam Scott. Always prepared."

Once the races started, us girls set up lawn chairs on top of the trailer to watch as the guys spent most of their time messing around with Kevin's race car and talking about "strategy." After Kevin's preliminary race, I could hear him and Mr. Scott using car jargon that I didn't actually understand to talk about problems with the engine and tires. I looked over at Kinsley who seemed to be entranced by what her dad and brother were doing. When she noticed me staring, she hopped out of her chair and knelt in front of mine. "Would you mind if I went down there to talk shop with my dad and brother?" With the way her face lit up as she asked the question, there was no way I was ever going to say no.

"Of course! Have fun." I smiled as I watched her excitedly head toward the ladder and climb down. Soon, she had joined her dad and brother, and all three of them had very serious expressions on their faces as they pointed to different parts of the car and studied them together.

Mrs. Scott sighed beside me. "This is so nice to see. I can't remember the last time I saw the three of them working together like that." She looked over at me, and it looked like she was trying to fight back tears. "I'm not sure what Kinsley told you about our relationship, but it hasn't always been the greatest. She's just so closed off. It's been that way since she was a teenager. She was such a fun loving child, and then she just lost it. I'm not sure what happened." She looked back down at her daughter, and this time, a few tears did fall from her eyes. "That's a lie. I know exactly what happened, and I blame myself for it every single day. She was a scared young girl with feelings that she didn't understand and felt like she had no one to turn to. She should have been able to turn to me, but I didn't know. I didn't want to see it because I didn't understand it. But all I did was push her away more, without even realizing it. I grew up in a different time, so I never knew gay people. All I had to go by were the negative things I always heard. So I repeated those things, never knowing that I was talking about my own daughter."

"And how do you feel about it now?" I asked the question quietly and hesitantly, sure that I was crossing a line that I shouldn't be.

Mrs. Scott sighed again, but this time it sounded more strained and she looked ashamed over what she was about to say. "It's a complicated feeling. I know that sounds terrible, but you have to understand. You kids are so open to all sorts of differences today. When I was growing up, people hid the things that made them different, so there was nothing to accept. I'm still trying my best to understand it. I just hope that my struggles with this don't hold her back from being that amazing girl that I know she's meant to be."

I looked down at Kinsley and watched as she threw her head back in laughter at something her brother had just said. I loved everything about the view - from the way one vein in particular in her neck popped more than others as she laughed to the way the lines from her smile seemed to travel all the way from her lips to her eyes. Kinsley was beautiful. Simply put, she was perfection. Without removing my eyes from her, I said my next words without reservation. "I'm going to be honest. Kinsley doesn't let people in much. Sometimes she pretends to be cold, just so she doesn't have to feel hurt or rejected. And truthfully, some of that *does* have to do with her worry over being rejected by her own family. But you don't have to worry about the person that Kinsley has become. Amazing can't even really be used to describe her because she's so much better than that. Kinsley is special. She's funny and smart, and she'd never admit it, but she cares a heck of a lot more than most people do. She's truly the most beautiful person I've ever met, inside and out." My face immediately started to burn with embarrassment when I realized I had just admitted that all out loud, and to Kinsley's mom on top of it all.

Mrs. Scott studied my face for what felt like hours, but I refused to make eye contact with her, worried about what I might find after that confession. I heard her take a deep breath beside me, then her voice took on a dreamy tone, as if she was lost in her own thoughts. "When you have a child, you fall madly in love from the very first moment that you hold them in the hospital. From that very moment, you dream of the exact life that you want them to have, and you know that no matter what life they choose - whether it is the one that you picture for them or not - that you're going to love them unconditionally through it all. From the time Kinsley was old enough to start dating, all I wanted was for her to find someone who looked at her the same way I did in the hospital all those years ago, and that's exactly how you look at her."

How was I looking at her, exactly? Clearly it wasn't the way you should look at someone who you were simply enjoying. "Oh umm.. we're not.. I mean.. we don't…"

Mrs. Scott patted my knee with her hand before my stuttering could continue. "Don't worry dear. You don't have to tell me anything. My own daughter doesn't even do that." She laughed playfully, and the rest of the night continued as though we hadn't both confessed more than we ever planned.

Once Kinsley and I had gotten into bed for the night, our mouths immediately began to get reacquainted. After a few minutes of making out, Kinsley pulled back and rested her forehead against mine. "I've been thinking about doing that all day," she admitted. She then ran a hand through my hair and placed a few soft kisses along my jawline, before looking at me again. "Did you have fun this weekend?"

I smiled, thinking back on the time we had spent with her family so far. "I did. It has been amazing getting to know your family and seeing how you interact in this kind of setting."

"You mean watching me fix a race car? Admit it - you thought that was pretty sexy."

"Oh I found it incredibly sexy," I whispered into her ear. I watched as Kinsley's eyes closed as I ran hand up and down her arm. There was so much that I wanted to talk about in that moment. I wanted to tell her about the talk that I had with her mom. I wanted to discuss the substitute teaching job I had applied to for the school districts in the Philadelphia area and how I had found a few apartments that I could rent that weren't too far from hers. I knew all of this could end up scaring her away. If she heard it, she might get the wrong idea about my expectations. *But was it really the wrong idea?* I could deny it all I wanted to, but I was falling hard and fast for Kinsley. I didn't want to just *enjoy each other exclusively.* I wanted more than that. I wanted commitment and a future and I wanted it with her.

Kinsley opened her eyes again and smiled up at me. "Are you thinking the same thing I am right now?"

I swallowed audibly. *Could it be?* "Depends. What are you thinking?" I did my best to keep my voice light and smooth, to keep from showing my nerves.

"Oh you know. Just thinking about how once we're back at the apartment, we should probably spend at least 24 hours naked to make up for the past two days." Of course that's what Kinsley was thinking. I'm not sure why I believed it would be anything different. Kinsley wasn't the type of girl who laid in bed and thought about her future, at least a future that went beyond the sexual happenings of the next 24 hours, and I couldn't expect her to be.

"I was thinking something like that," I lied. Although it wasn't a lie for long. Soon the thought of spending intimate time with Kinsley was the only thing on my mind.

By the time we made it to the door of the apartment the next day, it was taking everything in me not to rip her clothes off.

As I tried my best to unlock the door, Kinsley began to nibble on my ear. "You better hurry or my neighbors are going to get a show."

I pushed her away from me. "This would go much faster if you weren't distracting me."

We both laughed as we stumbled into the apartment together, surprised to see Leah pacing by the door. "I wanted to text you guys to warn you, but I didn't get the chance. She just got here. I didn't know what to do, so I let her in."

I was about to ask who she was talking about when I heard a door open down the hallway and watched for the person to emerge. A small gasp escaped me when a very familiar person entered the room. "Becky?!"

Chapter 19: Kinsley

Becky? As in *THE* Becky?! "What are you doing here?" I didn't miss the quiver in Grace's voice as she asked the question everyone was wondering.

"I need to talk to you. Grace, there is a ton I have to tell you. Could we... go somewhere please?"

Grace moved back a step, so she and I were standing side by side. "Anything you need to tell me, you can say in front of Kinsley."

I instinctively laced my fingers with Grace's. I was about to pull them away, but the feeling of her grabbing my hand tighter made me stay.

Becky looked toward our hands and then back up at Grace. "So, I take it that my suspicions were right? You already found yourself a new girlfriend. What happened to the girl who cried and told me that she would *never find another us*?"

Grace dropped my hand and took a few steps forward. "Kinsley and I... we're not... she's not my girlfriend." My heart dropped hearing those words just as it had the day I heard Grace say I wasn't her type. But why? It was the truth. We had agreed that we were just having fun.

"So, what is this then?" Becky asked, still looking back and forth between us. "Are you two just having sex or something?" She laughed as if this thought was preposterous. When no one responded, she scoffed. "Wow. Isn't this something? I guess people really do change." Her voice was dripping with sarcasm and judgment, and I didn't appreciate it.

I took a few steps closer to Becky. "Hey now. I realize this is none of my business, but given the circumstances, I don't think you have *any* room to judge."

To my surprise, Becky hung her head in response to my words. "You're right." She looked back up, but instead of pointing her eyes at me, she directed them toward Grace. "I didn't come here to fight with you. I'm sorry."

"So, why did you come here Becky?" Grace asked, her voice soft, yet stern.

"I ran into your mom the other day. She was with your niece, who told me how much she misses you by the way, and asked when you and I could take her to the park again. Anyway, your mom told me that you applied for a subbing position around here. I knew you gave up your position at our elementary school, and I've been beating myself up over that, but it hurts me even more to know that you are just going to be a substitute teacher now. You love having your own classroom and your own kids, but I do have some good news. I happen to know that a second grade teaching position is opening up for the spring back home. I'm sure if you told them you were interested, they wouldn't even accept applicants. You were stuck in kindergarten for so long, and your chance has finally come."

I tried my best to process everything she had just said. I had so many questions. Since when had Grace applied to be a substitute in this area? Why hadn't she shared that with me? I was also shocked to learn that Grace had a niece, but it hit me that there was a lot that I didn't know about Grace. I didn't know much of anything about her family. I definitely didn't know that she dreamed of being a second grade teacher. *Damn.*

My thoughts were interrupted by the sound of Grace's voice. "You drove all the way here to tell me that? You could have just called."

"That's not the only reason I'm here," Becky admitted. She took a few steps closer to Grace. "I came to say that I'm sorry." *More steps.* "And I made a huge mistake." *More steps.* "I should have never cheated on you." At this point, Becky was practically toe to toe with Grace. She reached out for her hand, but Grace quickly pulled it away. "Grace, I miss you. I miss us. I miss hearing about your day and eating dinner together. I miss spending time with your family. I miss touching you and feeling you close to me. I miss the way you used to hold me after we made love."

OK. I couldn't listen to this anymore. I cleared my throat, feeling like I couldn't breathe, and everyone in the room turned to look at me. "I think this is a talk that you two should be having privately." I turned toward Leah. "We should go." Before walking away, I reached out and squeezed Grace's hand. "I'll just be right in my room if you need me, OK?" She nodded slightly, looking completely shaken up, and all I wanted to do was lean in and kiss her. But now wasn't the time and I was starting to wonder if my time had run out.

Leah followed me down the hall and into my room, closing the door behind her. "Well, this is insane, isn't it?"

I didn't know how to respond. I couldn't even fully process what was going on. "Do you think I could just be alone?" I asked, angry at myself for how pathetic I sounded.

Leah nodded and turned to leave the room. Once she was at the door, she turned back around. "It's going to be OK, Kinsley. I promise. Grace cares about you." Sure. Grace *cares* about me. That didn't mean that I wasn't about to lose her.

"It's not about that," I lied. "I'm just tired from this weekend and need some rest." I was happy when Leah didn't push it any further and left without saying another word.

Unfortunately, just a few minutes later, there was another knock on my door. "Leah, I already told you that I need my rest."

Instead of leaving me alone, my door swung open. I was surprised to see Grace walk into the room. I quickly stood from my bed and walked over to her. Before I could overthink it, I wrapped her in my arms. Warmth overtook me when she melted into me as well. "Are you doing OK?" I whispered.

Grace pulled away, and I could see that she had tears in her eyes. "I'm OK. It's all just very confusing. She's saying all of the things that I was dying to hear up until just a few weeks ago."

I took her hand and pulled her over to sit on the bed next to me. "Where is she now?"

Grace nodded her head toward my door. "She's still out in the living room. She wants to go get dinner with me, but I told her I needed to talk to you first."

"Well, what do you want?" I asked, afraid to hear the answer.

"Honestly? I want to go back in time to just an hour ago when things felt a lot simpler."

I hated the fact that this didn't feel simple for her. I wanted her to go out and give Becky the middle finger, then spend the rest of the night in bed with me. But I didn't blame her for feeling confused. It took me years after Nikki dumped me to stop wishing that she would ask for me back. Even now after all this time, I had to wonder how my body would react to seeing her again. That's what happened when you thought you were going to spend the rest of your life with someone. If you had that life offered back up to you, it was completely normal to wonder if you should take it. The last thing I wanted was for Grace to have any regrets.

"You should go with her," I spoke, finally breaking the silence. "You owe her nothing. But you do owe it to yourself. I don't want you to always wonder what might have been."

Grace exhaled loudly beside me. "You're right." Instead of standing, she placed her hand on top of mine. "I know this is a strange request when I'm about to go to dinner with my ex, but could I have a kiss?"

Without saying a word, I captured Grace's lips with mine. It didn't take long for me to become completely enraptured in the kiss, letting all of the events of the past half hour to be forgotten. As our tongues developed a steady rhythm, Grace pulled me closer to her and we somehow ended up horizontal on the bed. I pulled my mouth away from Grace's and ran my tongue along her neck. When I heard Grace moan, I pushed my hand underneath her shirt, running it over her tight stomach until I reached….

Suddenly, I felt Grace's hands on my shoulders pushing me away. "Sorry, I think we got a little carried away there," she apologized.

"You mean you don't want to have a quickie while your ex is in the other room waiting to go to dinner with you?" I laughed, resorting to my old tactic of making crude jokes in order to avoid my feelings.

Grace gave me a look that told me she didn't appreciate the joke. "Please don't do that."

"Do what?" I asked, feigning innocence.

"Please don't act like a douche because you're upset."

I rested my head against Grace's. "I'm sorry. I guess this is all a little weird for me too."

Grace turned her body so our foreheads were touching. "I won't go if you tell me not to."

"You know that I'm going to do that. I want you to do this for yourself."

Grace nodded and actually stood up from the bed this time, leaving me alone with my thoughts once again. I sat motionless for a few minutes, before I noticed Lenny staring at me from his cage. "What dude? I'm allowed to be upset. I was supposed to be having sex, and instead, I'm sitting in my room while the girl I'm falling for goes on a date with her ex."

He continued to stare, and I groaned in response. "I get it. I told her to go. That doesn't make it any easier."

When he jumped from his perch and started running on the giant wheel in his cage, I rolled my eyes. "What did you expect me to do?! You think I should have told her not to go, don't you? I couldn't do that. She was so confused. She deserves to figure this out."

Lenny stopped running and stared at me again. "We're not actually together man. Remember? That was the deal."

I laid back down on my bed and shook my head. Is this really what my life had come to? I was talking to a chinchilla about my girl problems? After a few minutes of chastising myself, I must have drifted off to sleep, because when I opened my eyes, it was dark out, and someone was lying beside me on the bed. I blinked my eyes until Grace came into focus. She stared down at me as she ran a hand through my hair. "Did you eat anything?" she asked softly. "I brought some sweet and sour chicken back for you from that place a few blocks away that you love but never get since they don't deliver."

"That's where you guys ate?" I asked, unable to mask my disappointment.

"Of course not. I stopped there on the way back."

I couldn't help, but smile at this. "That was sweet of you. Where is Becky?"

"At a hotel. She apparently booked herself a room for the next week so she could have more time with me." Grace hesitated, then added, "Listen, we need to talk."

I felt a lump form in the pit of my stomach. I had heard those words before. Anyone who has ever been dumped has heard those words. Could this be considered being dumped though if we were never actually together? I couldn't bear the thought of being told that I wasn't good enough; that somehow a girl who cheats for six months straight is better than me. I had to take matters into my own hands, but did I really want to end things? Of course not. I enjoyed Grace too much for that. Maybe if I took a step back, we could keep things going for awhile. "You're right. We do need to talk. I'm sure you'll agree, but I think we should forget about the whole exclusive thing. That gives you more time to figure out whatever this is with Becky, and I can get back to the old me."

For a second, Grace faltered, and I thought maybe she would tell me that I read the situation wrong. "Oh..yeah...I mean, of course. That sounds like a good plan." *There goes that feeling again.*

"Perfect!" I answered a bit too enthusiastically. "I'm exhausted, but you're welcome to stay in here or go back to Leah's room. Up to you." I turned my back to her and willed myself not to cry. This was a good thing. What did I expect to happen anyway? It's not like I was going to actually let myself get tied down to one person. I wouldn't make that mistake again.

Chapter 20: Grace

As I laid in bed next to Kinsley, I stared up at the ceiling, wondering how things had gone downhill so quickly. Except, I knew exactly how that had happened. Becky had showed up in Philadelphia. Becky, the girl I thought I was going to spend the rest of my life with; the person I thought I could never possibly get over. I let my mind play back the events of the evening.

After leaving Kinsley's room, I came back to the living room to find Becky sitting on the couch waiting for me. She took one look at my flushed face and shook her head. "I have to say Grace, I'm kind of shocked that this is the girl you have become these past few months. You made me wait how long before we had sex? Over a year? Now you're hooking up with a girl who doesn't even want a relationship with you. It's cool if that's what you want to do. I just hope you haven't lost yourself."

I wasn't sure whether to feel angry or ashamed from her words. It wasn't like she had said anything untrue. But wasn't I allowed to change? Plus, Kinsley wasn't just some random hookup. I had real feelings for her. Feelings that were now being thrown for a loop since Becky was apparently back in the picture. Instead of acknowledging her accusations, I suggested that we head out. I took her to a small sports bar a few blocks away, purposely avoiding any place Kinsley and I had gone together.

We spent the first part of the meal immersed in small talk to avoid the actual topic. I was surprised how easy it was to fall back in rhythm with Becky. But then again, in the four years we were dating, she was more than just my girlfriend. She was my best friend too. She knew me better than anyone else, whether I liked it or not. After catching up on the latest small town gossip and discussing the lady hired to be the new kindergarten teacher, Becky became serious. "So, tell me the truth. What's the deal with this Kinsley chick?" I shrugged my shoulders, unsure how to explain what was going on between Kinsley and I. "Well, do you have feelings for her?" Becky pushed.

My heart fluttered as I thought about how I felt about Kinsley. "Yes. I have very strong feelings actually."

A hurt expression entered onto Becky's face. "But if you have feelings for her, why aren't you guys together?"

"It's complicated."

"Try me."

I groaned at Becky's persistence. "I wasn't ready for a relationship after everything that happened with you, and Kinsley…,Well, Kinsley doesn't do relationships."

Becky scrunched her face as if she was in deep thought about my words. "So, where is this going?"

I rolled my eyes to show my annoyance at her questioning. It felt like I was talking to my mom instead of my ex-girlfriend. "I don't know, Becky. We were just enjoying where it was at." It felt wrong to be discussing Kinsley with anyone other than Leah, so I decided to change the subject. "And what about Jamie? I thought she was your soulmate?"

"That ended a few weeks ago. I was kidding myself by being with her. I wasn't actually in love with her. I was trying just to convince myself that I hadn't messed up the best thing to ever happen to me for something that was nothing more than a fling."

I shook my head, trying to wrap my mind around what she was telling me. "Becky, you cheated on me with her for six months."

As if on cue, Becky broke down into tears. "I know! And I honestly have no good excuse for why I did that. I'm not sure if I was trying to sabotage something that seemed too good to be true or if I let my hormones get the best of me, but it was never anything more than sex for me. I never stopped loving you. I still love you, Grace."

I held onto my head. "None of this makes any sense, Becky. If you have always loved me, what made you decide to come here now?"

"Honestly?" Becky sniffled. "I saw your post with the picture of you and Kinsley and I knew I had to come fight for you if I wanted to have any chance of getting you back. Please tell me I still have a chance. I'm ready to start our future together. I want to get married. I want to have kids. I know you want all of those things too, and I'll do anything to prove that I mean it." Becky stared at me longingly as I tried to process what she was saying. "So?"

"So what?"

"Do I still have a chance?"

I wanted to say no. I wished I had no reservations about sending her packing and never seeing her again, but I couldn't do that. The truth was, if Kinsley actually wanted a future with me, I would choose her instantly. My feelings for her were exponentially stronger than any dwindling feelings I thought I might have for Becky. But I was a twenty-eight year old girl who wanted to settle down. I wanted all of those things that Becky was talking about, but I wanted them with a person who most likely didn't want them at all. As if reading my mind, Becky spoke up again. "You don't have to decide anything tonight. I know you're thinking about Kinsley. It's pretty obvious that you believe you have some pretty strong feelings for her. But just remember everything that I'm willing to give you. I'm ready to fight for the chance to make those dreams come true for you." She then gave me all of the information for the hotel she was going to be staying in and I excused myself so I could go back to the apartment.

I knew exactly what I had to do. I had to talk to Kinsley and tell her that I wanted more out of this relationship. I didn't want to just enjoy each other. I didn't want just sex. I needed to see if she could promise me the same future that Becky was offering. Somehow, as I walked home, stopping at the Chinese takeout place to get Kinsley her beloved sweet and sour chicken, I convinced myself that just maybe this could work with Kinsley. There was no denying that we had something special, so maybe that would be enough to change her outlook on love. These dreams were quickly shattered when Kinsley told me that she didn't think we should be exclusive anymore. I figured this was probably all part of Kinsley's defense mechanism since she didn't show any interest in exploring other options until Becky was back in the picture, but I still didn't see the point in confessing my feelings to her. What was the point in opening myself up just to get my heart broken all over again?

That brought me to this moment, lying beside Kinsley in her bed. My body was pressed up against hers, without even an inch of space between us, but I had never felt so far away from her. I knew that I wasn't ready to have things end between us, so I had no other choice than to be OK with this new arrangement. I closed my eyes, hoping I was able to get some rest. It seemed like I had barely fallen asleep when I felt her stirring beside me. Soon she rolled over so she was now facing me and wrapped her arms around my waist. Before her eyes even opened, she began kissing my neck, and I couldn't help the moan that escaped me, similar to the one from the night before. As she sucked on my pulse point, I tried my best to keep my thoughts straight. "Kinsley... don't... you think... we should... maybe... discuss some... some rules," I asked between gasps.

Kinsley quickly pulled back. "Rules?!" The confusion in her voice made me believe that she had forgotten our conversation from the night before. I watched as the realization hit her, but instead of the sadness that I expected to see, a smile spread across her face. "If we didn't have rules before, then we certainly don't need them now. We're free. We can do whatever the hell we want."

Her words were the opposite of a turn on, so I scooted out of the bed before we could continue with any extracurricular activities. I poured myself some cereal, then sat down on the couch, not even bothering to turn on the TV. A few minutes later, Kinsley emerged from the bedroom. "Dude, what's the deal? You left me high and dry in there. Emphasis on the dry."

I rolled my eyes at her choice of words. "I just don't like the way you're acting right now."

"Seriously, Grace? How do you want me to act?"

"I just want you to be the Kinsley that I have grown to know and…" I stopped myself before the next word could leave my mouth. Did I really almost say that out loud? "I just want you to be the Kinsley I know, OK?"

If Kinsley had noticed my little slip up, she didn't acknowledge it. "The Kinsley you know is an asshole. You've pointed that out plenty of times."

"Fine. But could you at least wait until I have my whole breakfast eaten before you start being an asshole?" I joked, finding it impossible to stay mad at her.

Kinsley smiled that thousand watt smile that made me completely forget about everything else. "Deal."

With that aside, Kinsley and I fell back into our normal routine for the next two days. I also successfully avoided seeing Becky. She called me a few times, but agreed to giving me the space I requested. In return, I gave her a list of places to explore in the city.

***

By Wednesday, I was starting to feel a little guilt over the fact that she was there for me and I refused to see her, so I agreed to get a happy hour drink with her.

Again, I found that casual conversation flowed easily between us. It actually felt like I was catching up with an old friend. "So, have you given any more thought to what I said?" Becky asked once she had a bit of liquid courage in her, throwing that whole illusion out the window.

Apparently my liquid courage came in the form of anger. I slammed my drink down harder than I meant to, causing it to spill all over the table. "You *cheated* on me Becky. I know I sound like a broken record, but you didn't *just* break up with me. You were seeing someone else for *six months* after we had been together for four years."

Becky's tears immediately returned, just like the other night. "I know! And I said I'm sorry. I know that's not enough, but I'm willing to do whatever I have to to make it up to you. I'll spend my whole life making it up to you."

I put my hand up for her to stop. "No. Stop. If there is any chance at all of this being a possibility, and I'm still not saying that there is, I need you to listen to everything I have to say." Becky's eyes widened in response to my words, but she kept her mouth shut. "You *cheated* on me for six months with someone who I thought was my friend. The whole time you were seeing Jamie behind my back, you were talking about our future as if we still had one. Then that day came that I found out about you guys because I literally walked in on her going down on you. And let me tell you something - the look I saw in your eyes that day wasn't one of regret or sadness. It was pure horror of getting caught. Even after that little display, I still wanted us to be together for some reason, but you were quick to run me out of the house. You pretty much ran me out of town as well. Do you know what it was like watching you be happy with someone else right in front of me, while my heart was breaking?"

"I do now," Becky responded softly. "That's exactly how I felt when I saw you with Kinsley. You were hooking up with her in the next room while I waited for you to come talk to me. Then you didn't even have the decency to fix your sex hair. But you know what? That's OK because I deserve it. I deserve for you to do that to me a thousand more times."

Her words stung. I didn't want to be that girl. The last thing I wanted to do was string two people along. It wasn't my intention. "I'm sorry if that hurt you, but I need to be honest with you, Becky. Just because I met with you tonight, doesn't mean that anything has changed with Kinsley."

"Does this mean you guys are going to make things official?"

That question hurt even more than her previous accusations. That's all I wanted with Kinsley, and instead, we were headed in the opposite direction. "Not that it's any of your business, but no, we're not official. But I'm also not ready to give up whatever it is that we have."

Becky reached across the table and grabbed ahold of my hand. She held it tight so I couldn't pull it away. "I respect that and want you to take all of the time that you need. But just remember... you and I have a past, and we can also have a future. Do you really want to throw that all away for a *right now?*"

I wasn't sure how to respond to this, but luckily Becky let it drop there. After finishing our drinks, I made the mistake of agreeing to let her walk me back to the apartment. When we arrived, I was happy to find that all of the lights were out. It made me wonder where Kinsley had gone, but I was just glad she could avoid an awkward run in with Becky. I flipped on the light, then turned to say goodbye to Becky, hoping she wouldn't try to stick around. Becky took a step closer to me. "I had a really great time tonight." Her words made it sound more like a date than a serious talk, but I decided to ignore that fact.

"Umm yeah.. goodnight Becky," I muttered.

When she leaned in for what I assumed was a hug, I decided to accept it, but to my surprise, her lips landed on mine. I pushed her away before the kiss could even happen and saw the immediate disappointment take over her face. After a second, she stood up straighter as if she were trying to gain back some dignity that she had just lost. "OK. Listen Grace. Here's the deal. I know I was supposed to stay a few more days, but having me here clearly isn't working for you. I think you need some actual space to really think about this.

But before I go, there's something else I need to tell you. I wanted to surprise you with this, but I won't be able to if you don't give me a chance, so I might as well just say it. Do you remember that fixer upper about a mile from your parents' house?"

Of course I remembered it. That house was on the market from the time I was in high school. No one wanted it since it was so rundown. For whatever reason, I always saw potential in it. As the years passed and it continued to sit uninhabited, I decided that I would buy it someday and fix it up. Unfortunately, I dragged my feet (mostly because when I started dating Becky and mentioned it to her, she stuck her nose up at the suggestion), and someone ended up buying it two years ago. I was heartbroken the day that the for sale sign was replaced with a sold sign, but I had no idea why Becky would choose to bring that up now. "Yes," I sighed. "Why are you asking about that now though?"

Becky's face lit back up. "It's back on the market. Apparently the guy who bought it did a decent amount of work on it, but had no intention of actually living in it. Rumor has it he bought it for one of his kids who ended up moving to another state. Who knows. The important part is that it's for sale again, and I'm going to put an offer on it. I want it to be our first house together. Maybe our forever home."

My head was spinning again. This had the makings of every romance novel I had ever read. Girl meets girl. Girl falls in love. Girls inevitably break up. Girl realizes the error of her ways and swoops in with the grand romantic gesture. There was one problem. It was the wrong girl, and I couldn't shake the feeling that this wasn't my story. "This is a lot to think about, Becky. That's a really sweet gesture, but I don't think you should do anything rash. Buying a house isn't something you just do on a whim. "

Becky grabbed onto my hands. "But I would do that for you. That's what I need you to know."

I dropped my hands back at my side. "It's just a lot, Becky."

"I know, I know. That's why I'm giving you space. But listen, school starts for me again in two and a half weeks. I'm not saying you have to make any decisions in that time, but what if you think things through, then come back home for a visit that weekend before things get crazy for both of us? Your mom told me that you haven't been home all summer, so if nothing else, at least you'll get to see your family."

"Becky…."

"You should do it," a voice came from behind me.

I turned around to see Kinsley standing beside the couch. She was wearing nothing but boxer shorts and a sports bra, and my mouth went dry at the sight. My heartbeat had also taken on a rapid pace. I didn't know if it was a reaction to how good she looked or the fact that she was in the room practically pushing me back into the arms of my ex. Regardless, I had to look away from her. The emotions were too much to take. When I looked back at Becky, she had a smug grin on her face. "*See!* Even *she* thinks it's a good idea."

I wanted to point out that *she* had a name, but I was too overwhelmed by the whole situation to say anything. Becky reached out and squeezed my hand. "Just think about it, ok?" She winked at me, then turned and walked back out through the door, leaving just me and Kinsley.

I walked over to the couch and threw myself onto it, closing my eyes as I laid down. To my surprise, I felt a pair of hands lift my glasses off my face. I looked up at the now blurry figure standing above me. "Can't have you breaking those," Kinsley explained. The sound of her voice told me that she was currently smiling. I didn't want her to be worried over the Becky situation, but it still hurt that she seemed to take it all so lightly. I closed my eyes again, unsure how I was supposed to react to any of this.

I heard Kinsley walk to the other side of the couch, where she lifted my feet so she could sit and put them back on her lap. I waited for her to say something, but she didn't. Instead, she gently ran her fingers back and forth along my legs. "Why did you say I should go home?" I finally asked.

Kinsley sighed as if I had just asked her the most obvious question in the world. "Home has what you want - your family, the teaching position, your dream house... Becky."

"There is one very important piece missing from all of that."

"And what is that?"

I growled in frustration. "It's you Kinsley! It's whatever this is between us. I'm honestly not sure what it is at this point, but I'm also not willing to give it up."

Instead of getting a response, silence took over the room. I wouldn't have even known that Kinsley was still there if it wasn't for the fact that my feet were resting on her legs currently. The silence was killing me, and I was about to speak up when she finally did. "Well, lucky for you... I am."

"You are what?" I asked, hoping I had misunderstood where she was taking this.

"I'm willing to give this up. Let's face it, Grace. It's not going anywhere. You're cool and smart and sexy as hell, and we've had a ton of fun. But I think it's run its course. Let's be honest. It was getting too real anyway."

I sat up on the couch and grabbed my glasses off of the coffee table. I had to see Kinsley's face. I had to know if she meant what she was saying. Unfortunately, she would barely even make eye contact with me. She stood from the couch and began walking out of the room. Before heading down the hall, she shook her head and turned around. I stood from the couch as well and held my breath as she made her way back toward me. I waited for her next move, willing to accept whatever it was. Much to my dismay, she placed a kiss on my forehead that was so brief it almost felt like I had imagined it. When she pulled back she whispered, "Take care of yourself Grace," then walked away again.

"Can't we at least talk about this?!" I yelled after her. The answer was given to me in the form of silence, a silence that continued through that week and the next. My knocks on her door were met with no answer. My attempts to talk were met with nothing but grunts and groans. It was like the Kinsley that I had known the past few months had just evaporated.

It was so heartbreaking that by the time the potential date of the weekend visit with Becky was just a few days away, I decided to do it. If nothing else, I figured it would feel good to get away. Plus, unlike Kinsley, Becky wanted me and she was making no secret of that fact. Since leaving, she had called me every single night, continuing to make promises about our possible future. The more complicated things seemed to get with Kinsley, the more tempting it sounded to fall back into something easy and known. Becky was so excited about my decision, that I almost felt guilty about how indifferent I was.

Even with how bad things had gotten, I wasn't willing to leave without talking to Kinsley. No matter how much she pulled away from me, I still cared about her, and I knew she cared as well. That Wednesday, just two days before my trip, I knocked on her door for what felt like the millionth time in two weeks. When she didn't answer, I tried to open it, but was disappointed to find that she had locked it. "Kinsley, please," I pleaded. "Listen I need to talk to you. I decided to go this weekend, but I can't do that without seeing you first."

To my surprise, Kinsley finally opened the door in response to my begging. As soon as I was inside her room, I took her in completely. She looked different somehow, almost more tired. Her eyes appeared heavy and they had rings around them, almost as if she had been crying. Of course, she still looked amazing. I don't think it was possible for Kinsley Scott to look anything but amazing, and it was taking everything in me not to just fall into her arms. She motioned for me to sit on her bed. When she sat down beside me, I noticed that her shoulders slumped. Against my better judgment, I put my hand on her chin and directed her eyes toward mine. "Are you ok?" I asked.

Kinsley forced a smile in return. "I'm just dandy."

I groaned at her lies. After all of the time it took to get Kinsley to open up to me, it had taken only a few weeks for her to completely shut me out again. "What's wrong, Kinsley? Do you not want me to go? Because if not, just say the word and I'll forget it all."

"Of course you should go," she answered more firmly.

"You do realize that this could change everything, right?" My words made my mind flash to my future and what it might look like. It looked... nice. It looked fine. But it didn't look like anything I had experienced the past few months.

"Hasn't it already changed?"

"My feelings haven't," I answered softly. "Have yours?" Kinsley didn't answer, but simply shook her head in return.

"Then tell me to stay, Kinsley," I urged.

"I can't do that," she responded through gritted teeth.

"And why not?! If we both like each other, why can't we go back to being together?"

"Because we were never together, Grace! God, what do you not understand about that?! What we had always had an expiration date."

"Fine Kinsley. I'll just see you when I get back I guess."

She was right. What we had did have an expiration date. Kinsley didn't want me in the same way that I wanted her. But there was someone who did, and that's why I was determined to make sure this weekend went well.

Two days later, I was getting into my car to start my drive when Leah pulled in beside me. She jumped out of her car and leaned up against mine. "Were you really going to leave your oldest, bestest friend without saying goodbye?" she mock scolded.

"I'll be back in two days. It's not like I'm leaving you for good."

"Not yet," she pouted. "But if things go well, you will be."

"That's the plan," I sighed.

"Could you please remind me once again why you are doing this?"

"I don't know, Leah. I guess I just feel like I should give it a chance. Becky wants to be with me. She wants to build a life and a future together, and I'm just supposed to give that all up for what exactly?"

"Oh, I don't know. True love. The person you actually want to be with."

"Listen, Leah, I know you have this fantasy about your two besties ending up together, but that's just not realistic with Kinsley. I mean, come on, she is the one who encouraged me to go this weekend. She clearly doesn't want me."

Leah rolled her eyes in response to this. "OK. You keep telling yourself that," she quipped.

"Kinsley is complex and beautiful and truly the most amazing person I've ever met, and if I could have a future with her, I would. But, the truth is, we just want different things."

Leah placed a hand on my shoulder. "Just do me a favor and don't settle. You deserve better than that."

I promised her I wouldn't. It couldn't be considered settling if you ended up with your first love, could it?

Chapter 21: Kinsley

I laid in my bed Friday night listening to music when I suddenly felt a hand slap the side of my head. I looked up to see Leah staring down at me. I took my headphones off and sat up so we were level.

"What the hell is wrong with you?" Leah groaned.

I smirked back at her. "Nice to see you too, buddy." That earned me another light smack in the back of my head.

"Answer my question. I asked what the hell is wrong with you."

I rubbed my head and glared back at her. "Well, right now I'm thinking it's the fact that I might have a concussion."

Leah rolled her eyes at me. "Stop. You know exactly what I'm talking about so don't play dumb with me. Why would you let Grace leave?"

I shrugged my shoulders. "Grace is a grown woman. She can make her own decisions."

"I just don't get it, Kins. We've lived together for like 7 years now, and I've never seen you as happy as you were in the two months Grace was here. I also know Grace. I know she wouldn't have gone if you told her not to."

I used my eyes to tell Leah that she needed to back off. "I'm not talking about this right now," I warned.

"Fine," Leah sighed, but instead of leaving, she sat down beside me on the bed and pushed her shoulder against mine. "Are you OK? Because you look like shit."

Of course I looked like shit. I had spent the last three weeks crying, but I would never admit that to Leah. Ever since Becky showed up, I felt like my entire world was falling apart. I did what I had to do for Grace though, and I could be happy knowing that. I just hoped some day she would realize

I did it all for her. Telling her that I didn't want her was the hardest lie I ever told, but that's what you do when…

"Are you crying?" Leah's voice interrupted my thoughts. I moved my hand up to my face and felt moisture on my cheeks. *Shit.*

"I've just been sick," I lied. "My sinuses have been acting up. That's why I haven't been around. Snot everywhere."

"Cool story, bro," Leah quipped. "If you ever decide to tell me the truth, I'm here to listen. But for now, what can I do to get you to smile again?"

For the first time in what felt like forever, a genuine smile spread across my face. "You could help me get laid."

Leah scrunched up her nose at my request. "It feels weird to support that when it could hurt my other bestie in the process."

"Seriously, dude?" I scoffed. "She's shacking up with her ex this weekend. Do you honestly think she's not getting it in?"

Leah stared at the ceiling as if she was considering my words. "Fine. When do you want to go?"

"Five minutes," I squealed, as I hopped out of bed.

Within an hour, Leah and I were walking into the club. As soon as I took in my surroundings, flashbacks started from the times I was there with Grace. They were so vivid that I could feel them. I felt her touch as we walked out of the bar that first night. I heard her gasp as I pushed her against the brick outside and kissed her for the first time. I remembered my shock when she admitted that she could only think about kissing me. I wanted it to be her here with me. I wanted to sweep her onto the dance floor and feel her body against mine. I wanted to kiss her as if we were the only two people in the room. I wanted to take her home and make love to her all night.

She wasn't here though. It was just me, Leah, and my broken heart. There was also tons of alcohol and enough single, desperate lesbians to have my choice of who to take home. "What's the game plan, boss?" Leah asked, interrupting my thoughts.

"Well, I figured we could start the night out with some tequila shots."

Leah made a face at my request. "So, it's that kind of night? Ok. Let's do it."

It certainly was that kind of night and before long, I could feel the effects of the alcohol buzzing through my body. Leah and I made our way to the dance floor and danced close as she started pointing girls out to me. I came up with reasons not to approach any of them - too gay, too straight, too short, too tall, too brunette, too blonde - the excuses were endless. Finally, Leah threw up her hands in frustration. "Do you actually want to do this or not?! Because I am more than fine with going to get pizza and calling it a night."

"Of course I want to do this. I'm Kinsley Freaking Scott." Yes I was. I could totally do this. I quickly scanned the bar and made a beeline for the first girl I made eye contact with. I couldn't even tell you what her hair color was or how tall she was. I was on a mission and nothing else mattered. Once I was close enough, I reached out and placed a hand lightly on her hip. "Dance with me?" It was somewhere between a question and a demand and certainly not my best plan, but it worked. Soon, she was pressed up against me, and I could feel myself becoming turned on. I watched as her auburn hair swept across her back, and when she turned to face me, I stared right into those green eyes and counted the freckles on her face. Only her eyes weren't green and there were no freckles adorning her face, at least not any I could see in the dark club. Her short blonde bob certainly hadn't been grazing her back just a moment ago. I slowly backed away as if I had just seen a ghost, bumping into a few people along the way, which earned me some glares. "I'm sorry. I can't do this," I muttered. I made my way out of the club as quickly as possible and took deep breaths as I leaned against the cold brick wall.

"What's going on?" a worried Leah inquired. She took my face in her hands and stared right into my eyes. "Kinsley, talk to me."

And just like that, the water works started. Like a drunken idiot, I broke into tears right in the middle of the Philadelphia gayborhood. I was acting like every drunk girl I had ever made fun of, but I couldn't bring myself to care. Leah threw an arm around my waist and started to walk with me. I didn't know if it was the alcohol or exhaustion from carrying so many pent up emotions, but I had to lean on her to stay upright. She slowly guided me all the way back to our place, and once we were back home, sat me down on the couch. She ran into the kitchen and emerged a minute later with a big glass of water. I sipped it slowly as she rubbed my back. After a few minutes the tears had finally subsided, for the most part at least. I was starting to think I had busted open some damn tear gland and would spend the rest of my life with some amount of liquid leaking from my eyes at all time.

Leah continued to run her hand over my back as she spoke softly. "Is this about Grace?"

I took another large sip of water. "Of course it is."

"You like her, don't you?"

I shook my head in response. "No Leah. I don't like her. I... I love her." I couldn't believe that I had just admitted that out loud. I hadn't even fully admitted it to myself yet.

A subtle, yet apparent, smirk entered onto Leah's face. "This is a good thing, Kins. You need to tell her."

I huffed. If only it were that easy. "She's with Becky right now, Leah. They are trying to work things out."

"Don't play dumb. You know perfectly well that if Grace knew you wanted to be with her, she wouldn't even be giving Becky a second thought."

"That's exactly why she can't know," I warned.

Leah tipped her head to one side. "I'm going to need you to elaborate please."

"Grace deserves to be with someone who is better than me."

"And you think that person is the girl who *cheated* on her?"

I shrugged my shoulders. "They have history. Becky lives in Leah's town. She already knows her family. I didn't even know that Grace had siblings before Becky mentioned her niece."

"She has an older sister and a younger brother. She only has the one niece. She's five. Now you know," Leah answered nonchalantly.

"That's not my point," I groaned. "The point is that I didn't even have the decency to find that out in the time we were hooking up. I'm not a good person Leah. I have hurt so many people that I care about because I can't get past my own insecurities. I couldn't stand the thought of hurting Grace."

"Here's an idea dork. Don't hurt her."

"I wouldn't do it on purpose. I just don't even think I know how to do an adult relationship. Becky wants to give her a house. She's ready to settle down and make a plan for life. I don't even like planning out what I'm going to eat the next day."

"I just think…"

I put my hand up before she could continue. "Just drop it, Leah. It's over. Time to move on."

Except I wasn't ready to move on. I laid in bed, staring at Grace's contact information in my phone, wondering if I should say screw it and just call her. When I woke up the next day to a spinning room and a massive headache, I found out that drunk Kinsley had other ideas. My eyes went wide as I studied the messages I had sent to Grace.

11:27 PM: Sorry I'm an ass
11:56 PM: Lenny misses you
12:02 AM: So do I
12:57 AM: Sorry I never asked about your family
1:23 AM: I hope your dreams come true
1:32 AM: And that we can still be friends
1:55 AM: Welp...Gonna puke...NIGHT

Seriously, Kinsley? What was wrong with me? At least I didn't drop the L bomb over text. Although, I did tell Leah. *Great. I would never hear the end of this.* I stared down at my phone again. It was now just after 9, and I hadn't gotten a reply to my late night rant. I was about to put my phone away when a new text message came through. As I read it, more followed.

9:07 AM: Hey Kinsley. I hope you're feeling ok after last night. Make sure you drink a lot of water.
9:10 AM: Also...Don't worry about it. All is forgiven.
9:13 AM: I'll always be your friend.

As I read the last text, I could feel tears hitting my face again. *Damn tear gland.* Sure, I had said the word friend first, but I wasn't sure how I was actually going to be Grace's friend. How was I supposed to listen to her go on about her wonderful weekend at home and help her move back out and watch her start a new life with someone else? The answer was simple. I couldn't do it. I had to get away. I knew exactly what to do. I was going to run back to the place and people that I ran away from to begin with.

Chapter 22: Grace

To say that I was surprised to wake up to a string of texts from Kinsley would be an understatement. Clearly she was drunk, but it was strange that her nightcap activities involved texting me. I read back over the texts for probably the hundredth time. I had woken about an hour ago and still hadn't figured out the right response. I decided to keep it light. There was no reason to spill my heart to a girl who was about to wake up with a massive hangover. Plus, Kinsley had said that she wanted to be friends. She had made it perfectly clear that she didn't want anything more from me than that. I finally sent back three texts explaining that I forgave her and would always be her friend. I couldn't imagine not having Kinsley in my life, so if friendship was my only option, I would take it.

I sat my phone back on the nightstand just in time to feel Becky stirring beside me. My first night back here had certainly been interesting. The apartment looked exactly as it had when I moved out, sans the items that I had taken with me. All of the pictures of Becky and I were back on display. I had to assume that was a recent addition in the past few weeks. I had arrived to find that Becky had made chicken parmigiana and spaghetti with the homemade sauce that I always loved. We then watched a movie and went to bed. I was hesitant to share a bed with Becky, feeling like I was somehow cheating on Kinsley. I had to remind myself that we weren't together and weren't ever going to be. Becky naturally spooned me from behind as this had been how we always fell asleep. It was comfortable being snuggled up against her. I liked the safe feeling of being close to someone. Granted, it didn't compare to having Kinsley's strong arms wrapped around me. I scolded myself for having these thoughts as Becky opened her eyes and smiled over at me.

"Good morning," she yawned. "I guess we should get up. I made an appointment to see that house before lunch."

Within an hour, we were walking into the house that I had admired from the outside for years. It was much less of a fixer upper than it had been. The previous owner did a lot of work on it, but I could still find plenty of changes to make. "It looks like there are a lot fun projects for us here, huh?" Becky asked, reading my mind. I just nodded in response, continuing to take in my surroundings. Becky's smile grew as she pointed to my glasses. "Since we're going to be doing so much manual labor, maybe we can finally get you in some contacts."

"I like my glasses," I pouted. "Some people may even call them sexy." My mind flashed to Kinsley once again.

"You're adorable darling, but I don't think anyone would call those glasses sexy," Becky snickered. "Anyway, shall we go? We have lunch plans."

I lifted an eyebrow as we walked toward the car. "Lunch plans?"

"Yes! With Kim Schulman."

The principal? "Kim Schulman as in Principal Schulman?"

Becky looked at me as though I was crazy. "Obviously, silly. How many other Kim Schulman's do you know? She was very excited when she heard that you were most likely coming back to town and are interested in the teaching position."

I wanted to point out that none of this was a definite, but I decided to keep it to myself. Things were going well, so I didn't see any reason to stir the pot at this point. As soon as we made it inside the restaurant, Principal Schulman wrapped me in a big hug. "Honey, it's so good to see you. We all knew you wouldn't be able to stay away for long. I was sad to hear that Jamie would be leaving, but we are excited to possibly have you back in the elementary school."

Of course it was Jamie's job that I was taking. Apparently, Becky had run her out of town too. I tried not to think about this as I smiled over at Principal Schulman. "Nothing has been decided for sure yet, but if I do end up back here, that second grade position would be a dream for me."

After lunch, Becky suggested that we take a walk down by the river. After walking for a bit, she stopped and smiled over at me, taking my hands in hers. "Do you remember this spot?"

As I looked around us, my memories flashed back to that day about four years prior. Coming back to this spot used to make butterflies take flight in my stomach. Today the memories made me smile, but the feelings were long gone. "Of course I remember," I finally spoke. "This is where we first said 'I love you.'"

Becky squeezed my hands, then let go and playfully poked me in the side. "I still can't believe that I had to be the first to say it."

I shrugged my shoulders. "I was nervous. I obviously felt it. I mean, I said it right back."

Becky's face became serious and she turned her head slightly. "Do you still feel it?"

I finally did get a feeling in my stomach, but this was more of a pit than butterflies. "I'll always care about you, Becky, but I'm sorry. I'm not in love with you anymore."

Becky's face dropped for only a moment before she was smiling again. "Well, that's OK. We can get there! No matter how long it takes, I will wait for you. And even if you don't get back to that point, would it really be so bad? I mean, we can still be happy and have all of our dreams come true."

I simply smiled back at Becky. A year ago, all of my dreams seemed so clear. Now I wasn't so sure what it was that I wanted. Well, I was sure of one thing, but that particular thing wasn't happening.

Later that night, Becky and I went to my parents' house for family dinner. My family was cordial to her, but they were far from warm. I tried to ignore this since it was nice to have this time with them again. As Becky and I did the dishes, my mom walked up behind me and laid a hand on my back. "Honey, I was wondering if it was possible for us to get lunch tomorrow, just the two of us."

"I think that's a wonderful idea, Mrs. Harper," Becky answered before I could. "You guys could even turn it into a weekly tradition once Grace moves back home."

Satisfied with her answer, Becky smiled and turned back toward the dishes. I could tell by the way my mom was looking at her that she probably shouldn't be so happy about it.

This was the same look my mom gave me when I sat across from her at lunch the next day. She sighed and reached for my hand. "I'm not going to waste time with small talk. What's going on, Grace? Don't get me wrong. I'm so happy to have you home, but why are you suddenly back playing house with Becky as if you two never broke up?"

I stared down at the table. "We're just giving it another try."

My mom put her hand underneath my chin, forcing me to look up at her. "And what happened to Kinsley?"

I was confused by her question. I had barely shared anything about Kinsley with her. I had mentioned that she was Leah's roommate and that we had become friends, and I told her about my visit to Kinsley's hometown, but aside from that, I had kept the details of our relationship from my mom. "Kinsley and I were never in a relationship, and it's become pretty obvious that there is no chance of that ever happening in the future," I answered truthfully.

"Hmm…" my mom muttered, in that mom way that told me she wasn't buying a word I was saying. "That's too bad. Pam and I could have sworn that you two were endgame."

Pam? I had only ever met one Pam in my entire life and that was Kinsley's mom. To say that I was confused would be an understatement. "OK. I have so many questions right now. The first one being how you know the term endgame."

My mom laughed as if this was a silly question. "Oh honey.. you used to put those little things on your tumble blog thingy. Those stories. What did you call them? Fan fictions? You always talked about how the characters in them were endgame."

My mother not only looked at my Tumblr, but also read my fanfiction? Well, that's rich. "OK. I'm not even going to comment on that right now. I have too many other questions. Like how did you and Mrs. Scott somehow decide that Kinsley and I were endgame during your five minute conversation?"

My mom laughed even harder now. "Don't be silly, sweetie. Obviously we didn't decide that during a five minute conversation. That would just be crazy. I asked for her phone number during that conversation, and we came to that conclusion during one of our nightly chats."

What… the… "You're telling me that you have been talking to Kinsley's mom ever since my visit a few weeks ago?"

"Yes. Is that a problem?" She asked the question so nonchalantly, as if your mother becoming besties with the mother of the girl that you had essentially been friends with benefits with, was the most normal occurrence in the world.

"I mean… I guess not," I mumbled. "It's just surprising."

"Pam and I understand each other. We are both small town mamas who love our daughters, but have struggled to come to terms with our daughters being gay."

I rubbed my hands over my temples. "Let me get this straight. You guys went from talking about your struggles with having gay daughters to deciding that your gay daughters should be together forever?"

My mom pulled my hands away from my head and smiled at me. "We just think that you guys are good together."

Who was this lady, and what had she done with my mother? She had been accepting of my relationship with Becky, but she was certainly never overly excited about it. She definitely didn't have extensive conversations with her mother about how we were meant to be. "Mom, you've never even met Kinsley," I pointed out, stating the obvious.

She again laughed at my words as if I was being silly. "I haven't, but Pam has told me all about the way you two interact. I think that lady adores you almost as much as her daughter does. I can tell that you really like her too. I might even dare to use another 'L' word." She smirked while lifting one eyebrow.

I could feel my face turning red from her words. I'm not sure what was affecting me more: the fact that my mom mentioned both Kinsley and her mom adoring me, or the way she was able to figure out how I was feeling. "How could you know that, mom? You've barely even heard me talk about Kinsley," I argued.

"Seriously, honey? You found a way to bring up Kinsley in every single conversation we had this summer." I thought back on our conversations and realized that she did have a point, but none of that really mattered anymore.

"It doesn't matter how I feel, mom. Kinsley doesn't want me." I tried my best to keep my voice level as I said these words so my mom wouldn't realize how much it was killing me that this was the case.

"Well, I really doubt that's true. But regardless, why get back with Becky when your heart is clearly somewhere else?"

I let out a frustrated sigh. Apparently she wasn't going to let this drop. "Becky and I have a past, mom. She was the first girl I ever fell in love with. I really thought that we were going to be together forever and now I'm getting that chance."

"Yet you're talking about forever as if it's a death sentence, rather than a destiny."

"I'm almost 29 years old mom. I'm ready to settle down. I can have that with Becky."

My mom studied me for a moment before speaking again. "Do you remember what you said after you came out to me?"

"Don't blame the liberal media?"

"Probably, but that's not what I'm referring to," my mom chuckled. "After you told me, I was obviously having a tough time, and I stupidly asked if you would consider being with a guy just to make things easier on everyone. I'll never forget what you told me. You said, 'Mom, I could probably live a happy, comfortable life with a guy, and it would be just fine. But I don't want a fine life. I want the kind of life that they write fairy tales and romance novels about. I refuse to settle.' I guess I'm just wondering what happened to that girl."

It took everything in me to keep myself from crying. That girl got cheated on and thought that she would never move on. Then she met someone who not only put her heart back together, but also caused her to feel more than she ever had before, only to have that person also decide that she wasn't good enough. "She doesn't want me, mom." This time a few tears did fall from my eyes.

My mom moved from her seat and sat down beside me, pulling me in close to her. "Whether you end up with Kinsley or not, I still think you should be careful about jumping back into things with Becky."

"It's one weekend mom. I haven't decided anything yet."

"Just promise me that you won't settle. I want you to get your fairy tale, even if you have to wait for it."

Later that night, I was determined to make myself feel more for Becky. My mom was right. I didn't want to settle, but I was still hoping that I could make it work with her. As we watched a movie, I snuggled close to her on the couch. When it ended, I turned to face her, hoping that looking into her eyes would cause even the slightest flip in my stomach. As I stared into her eyes, Becky's own eyes moved to my lips, and she slowly leaned forward. Her closeness did cause certain feelings to arise, but I wasn't sure if it was excitement or just nerves. Her lips touched mine, and it felt nice. Connecting with someone on this level was always a good feeling. Becky ran her tongue across my lips, and I reluctantly opened my mouth to hers, and then I felt it - the longing in my gut; the hollow longing to be somewhere else, with someone else. I pulled back and shook my head. "I'm sorry, Becky. I can't do this."

"This is about *her,* isn't it?" I tried my best to ignore her snide tone.

"It's about us, Becky. When you cheated on me, I thought my life was over. Then I went to Philly, and it finally felt like I was living again. It made me realize that we had lost that spark a long time before we broke up. I mean, come on Becky, why do you think you felt the need to cheat on me? You were searching for that passion we had lost. It was a crappy way for you to go about finding it, but still. It's not fair to either of us to keep pursuing this."

When Becky didn't respond, I told her I was going to leave. She remained silent as I packed my bag up again. Once I was ready, I gave her a hug and turned to leave. "She's never going to be with you," Becky finally spoke. "I've known plenty of girls like Kinsley. She's not going to settle down and, even if she did, it wouldn't be with a girl like you."

I simply smiled at Becky in return. "I told you. This isn't about Kinsley. It's about me." And it was about me. It was about the person I wanted to be and the new dreams I wanted to pursue. Still, as I drove, my heart beat fast in anticipation of seeing Kinsley again. I missed her so much, and even if we couldn't be together, I still needed her in my life. As soon as I was in the apartment, I yelled her name, praying she was home. I walked into her room and was disappointed to find that she wasn't in there. "Where is your mama, Lenny?" I asked the cage that I now noticed was empty. I walked over to his cage and searched it.

"I'm really sorry, Grace." Leah's voice behind me made me jump. When I turned around, she handed me a note. "She wrote me one too, but it's not nearly as cryptic as yours."

I read the words in front of me. *Grace, I hope your future holds everything you wish for. I'm so sorry I can't be part of it. I meant everything I said. - Kinsley.*

Leah put a hand on my shoulder. "According to my note, she needed to spend some time back in her hometown with her family. I honestly have no clue what your note means, and I'm sorry." She didn't have to know. I knew exactly what it meant, and I wasn't sure if my heart could handle it.

Chapter 23: Kinsley

I was awoken Monday morning to the sound of loud knocking on my bedroom door. Before I could even bring myself to open my eyes, my mom came in. Much to my dismay, she tore the covers right off of me.

"Seriously, Mom?" I groaned. "What if I had been naked?"

She simply waved one hand at me. "I'm your mother. It's not like it would be anything I haven't seen before. Now get up. We need to talk."

"Talk?" That wasn't a word that I had heard from my mom much growing up. We usually just avoided the important topics until they went away.

"Yes. Talk. Something we should have done a long time ago. Listen, I'm so happy to have you home, and the fact that you brought Lenny tells me you're planning to stay for awhile, but I'm worried about you. You've never been one to run toward things, only away from them. So, tell me. Does this have to do with Grace?"

"Of course not. Why would this have anything to do with Grace?" I lied.

"Sweetheart, I saw the way you two acted around each other. I know she wasn't just your friend."

"It doesn't matter what she was," I sighed. "It's over now."

"Why is it over?" my mom pushed.

"She is getting back with her ex, and that's that," I answered as casually as possible.

My mom sat down on my bed next to me and leaned her back against the headboard. "I find that awfully strange since that girl was clearly smitten with you. Why would she go back to her ex?"

"Because I told her to, OK?" I snapped. "Can we just drop it?"

My mom shook her head. "That's the thing. I can't just drop it this time. I failed you way too many times by not talking to you. I'm not doing that again. So, tell me why you would tell her to go back with her ex when you clearly want to be with her."

"She deserves better than me. I've made a lot of mistakes and hurt a lot of people. I've let down the most important people in my life."

"Oh sweetheart. Did you ever think that maybe they let you down? Your grandma seemed to think that was the case."

I sat up at the mention of my grandma. "What do you mean?"

"After you went away to college and never came back to visit, she blamed your father and I. She said we should have done a better job of showing that we accepted you, and she was right."

"But you didn't know that you had anything to accept."

"Oh come on. Of course we did. We just refused to see it. You chose a random college in Wisconsin without even visiting it, and then spent all of your time with your roommate until suddenly you didn't." She took my hand in hers and squeezed it. "I truly am sorry that I let you down."

I shrugged in response. "We let each other down. At least you and I can make it up to each other. I'll never get that chance with grandma." I could feel the tears coming now, and there was no way I was going to stop them.

I leaned into my mom as she held me close. "Oh, honey. You never let your grandma down. All she ever wanted was for you to be happy. She was so proud of you, and I know she would be even more proud today." She paused for a moment, then added, "And now that we've established that, I think it's time for you to win your girl back."

I wiped the tears from my eyes and chuckled a bit. "I don't think so mom. I think I need to call it a loss and try to move on. I've never been one for big romantic gestures. I just can't do it."

My mom stood from the bed and reached down to squeeze my shoulder. "Have you ever thought that maybe Grace doesn't want the big romantic gesture? Maybe she just wants you." She turned to walk away, but turned back after a few steps. "Just think about it," she said with a wink.

I did think about it. I couldn't stop thinking about it. Long after my mom left, I laid in bed still thinking about our talk. It hadn't been easy to talk about all of that, but it felt good to finally have it off my chest. It seemed like I had turned over a new leaf, and I knew it was time for a change, whether that change brought me Grace or not. I wanted to be the person that Grace deserved, but all she had ever asked was for me to be myself. That's when it hit me. I knew exactly what I needed to do. I grabbed my phone, then heard another knock on my door. "Honey, I'm going to do some volunteer work at the library," my mom shouted from the other side. "I need you to get out of bed so you can lock the door when I leave."

I groaned, but hopped out of bed. "Seriously, mom? I don't even lock the door to my apartment in Philly all the time. What do you think is going to happen?"

When I opened my bedroom door, she was still standing on the other side. "You can never be too safe," she said in a sing song voice. I rolled my eyes and followed her to the front door, locking it as soon as she was outside, knowing very well that she would be listening for the sound.

I sat down on the couch and pulled my phone back out, pausing for just a moment before opening the Twitter app. I hit the button for a new tweet, then began typing, hoping and praying that Grace still had her notifications turned on for Laurel Lake.

Warning: Long thread coming. To all of my loyal fans - I think it's about time that I owe you all the truth. I've been a fraud. I write romance novels, but for many years now I have hated love. All of my posts talking about finding true love were a hoax - at least I thought they were. I'm still not a firm believer in happily ever afters (I'm not naive enough to believe that love can somehow keep bad things from happening...sorry) and I'll never be a hopeless romantic, but I have learned that we can all experience our great love story. I should know because I recently experienced mine. My only hope is that I didn't realize it too late. Grace - If you're reading this, I'm sorry. I'm sorry I pushed you away. I'm sorry I acted like I didn't care. I'm sorry for all of the times I was a complete asshole and for the countless times I'm sure I'll be an asshole in the future if given the chance. I never expected to feel this way. I never knew a heart like mine could fall for a heart like yours. You are like the shades to my sunset. You protect me even when I think I don't need it. I've been fighting this ever since I met you, but I don't want to fight it anymore. I love you Grace and I'm begging you that if there is any chance that you feel the same way, please don't give up on me. I'm finally ready.

I threw my phone on the couch and walked away from it. I wasn't ready to see what kind of response I would get. I had no idea what my readers would think about that post, and I certainly didn't know how Grace would react. Was it too late? Did she even feel the same way? I walked into the kitchen and poured myself a glass of water, hoping it would somehow dampen my anxiety. I was about to take a sip when I heard the doorbell ring. I rolled my eyes as I walked over to answer it.

"Mom, did you forget your keys again? I told you it was stupid to..."

I lost all train of thought when I opened the door and found Grace standing there. Her hair was pulled into a loose ponytail and she adjusted her glasses as she looked up at me with those big green eyes; those beautiful eyes. I wanted to say something, but words were escaping me. Luckily, I didn't have to be the one to speak.

"I love you too." Grace's words hit me so hard that I thought I might have to grab onto something to stay upright.

"Y-You do?"

Grace reached out and ran a finger along my cheek. "Of course I do, Kinsley. You're..." She paused and let out a contented sigh. "You're everything."

I couldn't believe what was happening. The girl that I had somehow fallen in love with was standing in front of me telling me that she loved me too. Something didn't add up though. "Wait. I wrote that tweet like five minutes ago. How are you here already?"

A look of confusion took over Grace's face. "Tweet? What tweet?"

What was going on here? *Leah. Damnit.* "She told you, didn't she?"

Grace just laughed at my confusion. "Kinsley, no one told me anything. I figured it out on my own."

"But how?"

More laughter. "You're not so hard to figure out, Kinsley Scott. You ran away. As soon as I saw the note, I knew you felt the same. You only run away when you care way too much." Her face became serious, and she pushed a finger into my chest. "But just for the record, that ends now."

I directed her arms around my neck and placed my hands on her hips. "I'm not going anywhere." Without hesitation, I pulled her in closer to me and used my mouth to make all of the promises I couldn't say out loud.

After a few minutes, Grace pulled back and rested her forehead against mine. "I believe you said something about a tweet."

She pulled back completely and reached into her purse, retrieving her phone and unlocking it to read the words I had written. I held my breath as her eyes scanned the screen. When she finally looked up, she had tears in her eyes. "Kinsley... that was... Ugh." Instead of continuing, she pulled me close again and began placing kisses along my jawline and then my neck.

"Grace, I meant every word. I want it all with you. I want to learn everything about you. I wanna meet your family. I want to be part of your forever. I'm never going to be someone who makes big romantic gestures, and I know that I'm going to mess this up a bunch of times. It won't be perfect, but I'll always fight for you. I just..."

Grace stopped kissing me to look up at me. "Are your parents home?"

"No. My dad is at the shop, and my mom is volunteering at the library."

Grace's smile became a smirk. "This is probably one of the only times you're going to hear me say this, but I really need you to stop talking."

"Oh? Oh!" I wiggled my eyebrows and scooped Grace up in my arms, carrying her into the house and toward our future.

Epilogue: Kinsley

"I'll get it," I shouted, hopping off of the couch to run to the door. "Thanks Frank!" I beamed. I grabbed the pizza and sat it on our coffee table.

Grace walked into the room and grabbed a plain slice of pizza from the box that was half plain, half meat lovers supreme. "Was that Frank?" she asked. "He's my favorite."

I watched as my girlfriend of two years flopped down on the couch and motioned for me to come join her. It's crazy how much can change while also staying exactly the same. Just a few months after Grace and I became official, Leah announced that she was going to move out of our apartment, which ended up coinciding perfectly with a job offer Grace had received for a third grade teaching position. The job was in a town about 30 minutes outside of the city and after moving there, Grace and I quickly agreed that we both preferred suburban living to city life and small towns.

"Shall we take a selfie for the gram?" I asked, as I leaned close to Grace and held up my phone. It turns out the Laurel Lake Twitter confession had only made me more popular, and my fans loved seeing pictures of Grace and I together, so I tried to give them what they wanted.

Grace laughed as she looked at my post. "You *would* make that the caption," she teased.

I tore my phone away from her in mock offense. "Hey! *Sunset and shades* is kind of our thing now. It expresses all of the feelings that are hidden deep within my heart," I answered sarcastically.

Grace shook her head at me. "I should have never admitted that to you." After I referred to that phrase in my big twitter confession, Grace had told me that, when she had written that caption on our first photo together, there were a million other things she wanted to say instead. She had specifically said she had wanted to 'express all of the feelings that were hidden deep within her heart' at that time, but decided to go with that so she didn't scare me away. Now I used it as a way to get out of saying anything overly romantic.

When she continued to pout, I leaned in and kissed her. "You know I love you."

"Why don't you show me just how much you love me?" Grace asked as she wrapped her arms around my neck and pulled me on top of her. Any other time I would have graciously accepted this offer. In our two years together, the sex was one thing that hadn't changed at all, unless you counted the fact that it somehow just kept getting better. But I had other plans tonight.

"Can't right now," I answered, pushing Grace off of me. "It's game night. Time for me to beat you at Scattergories."

Grace groaned. "Really? First of all, you've never once beaten me at Scattergories and as much as I love winning all of the time, do we really have to play that tonight? We always fight when we play, plus I feel like we have all the cards memorized at this point."

I smirked over at her. "Lucky for you, I found some new category cards online and printed them out."

Grace laughed and lifted an eyebrow at me. "Wow. And people say that *I'm* a dork."

"You *are* a dork," I corrected her. "But you're my dork and I love you."

Grace rolled her eyes and picked up the dice with the letters on it. "Fine. Let's do this."

I grabbed the dice out of her hands. "It's my turn to roll."

I threw the dice hard enough for it to roll right off of the coffee table and under a chair. I picked it up and sat it on the table with the letter "K" showing.

"That was super shady," Grace pointed out. "Are you trying to cheat?"

I scoffed at her accusations. "If I was trying to cheat, would I really choose one of the worst letters in the game?"

Grace studied me for a minute, then threw her hands in the air. "Whatever. You're never going to beat me, even if you do cheat."

I smirked at my beautiful girlfriend. "Trust me. I have no question that I'm going to be the winner this time."

"We'll see about that," Grace joked as she reached out and turned the timer over.

Instead of looking down at my own card, I focused on the girl next to me. Grace was laser-focused, chewing on her pencil and pushing her glasses back up her nose every few seconds. I found her perfect in every way possible and it was killing me to wait for her to figure out what was happening.

———Grace———

I studied the category card in front of me and wondered where the heck Kinsley had found it. *Pizza toppings, types of Chinese food, ways to get over an ex...* I continued to scan down to the bottom of the card. *Something you borrow, something blue.* I gasped as my eyes landed on the last category. It couldn't be, could it? Was this seriously happening? The words seemed to pop off of the page at me: *Name of a girl who wants to marry you.*

Tears were already starting to fall when I looked up and saw Kinsley down on one knee in front of me. I could tell by the glisten in her blue eyes that she was also trying to hold back tears. Kinsley pulled the ring out of the box she was holding and took a deep breath. "So, here's the thing. About two years ago, you put this hold over me. It's a sex hold, and I don't want to have sex with anyone else for the rest of my life."

I started to laugh through my tears. "Are you seriously proposing to me using this speech?"

Kinsley looked at me as though I was crazy. "Do you mean am I seriously proposing by bringing up one of the first conversations we ever had together because I'm romantic AF? Then the answer is yes." She smiled at me in the way that still made me go weak in the knees. "So, what's your answer? Will you marry me?"

I stood and pulled Kinsley up with me. "Yes! Of course I'll marry you!" I wrapped my arms around her neck and kissed her a few times, before she pulled back and used a shaky hand to slide a beautiful engagement ring onto my finger. I admired it quickly, before pulling her back in to resume kissing. Kinsley had just pulled me in tighter when there was a knock on the door and loud voices on the other side.

I pulled back and lifted an eyebrow at her. "You told our mothers about this, didn't you?"

Kinsley rolled her eyes. "I asked *my* mom for help picking out the ring, and she, of course, told your mom since they're besties. Then they insisted that I let them come."

"Kinsley Laurel Scott, answer this door now," Mrs. Scott's voice boomed from the other side.

"Yes, listen to your mother," another voice piped in.

"Leah too?" I laughed.

"Yes! Leah too, you asshole," her voice shouted from outside.

Kinsley laughed as she reluctantly pulled away from me and opened the door for them. Tons of shouting and hugs ensued as soon as they were inside. When the initial excitement finally wore off, we all sat around talking about the proposal and already discussing wedding plans (thanks to our mothers).

"Now you guys have to fight over which one of you has me as your matron of honor," Leah joked. She had chosen to have two maids of honor in her wedding with Liam just a few months prior.

"She's all yours," Kinsley shrugged. "I already decided that Lenny is going to be my chin of honor." Her face became serious, and she added, "he's also going to be the ring bearer. I hope that's ok."

"You got it, babe," I agreed. I was just excited that Kinsley wanted to marry me. She could have said that she was going to walk down the aisle wearing a chinchilla costume, and I still would have been OK with it, as long as it meant that I got to spend the rest of my life with her.

After a few hours, our mothers announced that they were going to go back to the hotel they were staying in for the weekend (thank God), and Leah followed suit, announcing that she better get home to Liam. Once they were gone, I took Kinsley back into my arms and leaned my forehead against hers. A sigh left my lips as I stared into the beautiful eyes of my perfect fiancée, feeling more love than I had in my entire life. "And they lived happily ever...."

Kinsley pulled back and pointed a stern finger at me. "Don't you dare say it."

I threw my head back in laughter, so thankful that this crazy (and slightly infuriating) girl was mine. "Sunsets and shades, babe. Sunsets and shades."

Acknowledgments

I wanted to give a big thank you to all of my beta readers who helped in producing the final draft of this book. I am filled with gratitude for all of your hard work and dedication. A special thank you to Ivy for helping me out along the way. Your constant encouragement and input made this book possible.

Thanks again to my beautiful wife for putting up with me while I wrote this. I know that I was in my own world most of the time and I appreciate the fact that you didn't kill me for that.

And to all of my readers - thank you so much! I can't even begin to put into words how much your support means to me.

About the Author

Erica currently resides in Pennsylvania with her wife, dog, bunny, and chinchilla. She spends her days checking eyes and her nights snuggled up with her furry family.

Connect with Me:
Follow me on Twitter:
http://twitter.com/EricaLeeAuthor

Follow me on Instagram:
http://instagram.com/EricaLeeAuthor

Visit my website:
http://astoldbyeri.wixsite.com/ericalee

Email Me: EricaLeeAuthor@gmail.com

Printed in Great
Britain
by Amazon

31392364R00132